The Dragon's Secret

An AdventureQuest Novel

By Lyra Trice Solis

Cover Art

Miltonius (Milton Poole)

Illustrations

Thyton (Alfonso ElJaiek)

Based on the hit games at

www.BattleOn.com

The Dragon's Secret

Visit the AdventureQuest website at www.BattleOn.com.
Visit the Artix Entertainment portal website at portal.battleon.com.

For questions or comments, please visit our forums at http://forums2.battleon.com.

ACKNOWLEDGMENTS:

Front and back cover art by Milton Pool.
Interior illustrations by Alfonso ElJaiek.

Artix Entertainment, LLC wishes to thank the following people:

The entire novel team: Tony Deller, Adam Bohn, Paresh Patel, PJ Beemer, Alicia Coburn, William B. Donges, Matt Wester, Sarah Stephens, Ray Stephens, Daniel Beeler, Luke Gamble, Jill Wong, Courtney Nawara, JP Gagnon, and all of the players who fought in the Great Fire War.

ISBN 978-1-4507-3404-2
Printed in Korea.

Dedication and Acknowledgments

This book is dedicated to Chuck, my own personal hero: He's never been to Lore, but without him, this book would not be possible. And for the rest of the gang: Ray, Sage, Kenne and Autumn, who help keep my kid-juice up.

Some people do everything they do with their whole hearts, and never worry about what's in it for them. Aelthai is one of those people. She's gone out of her way to patiently answer at least a bajillion questions, and to find answers when I didn't know where to look. Galanoth's enthusiasm for this tale of his young protégé is matched only by his enthusiasm for killing dragons, and he is truly a hero in my book. Razer, your sense of fun kept me going, and kept a smile on my face. Could any book be written about Lore without the wise counsel of Falerin, loremaster extraordinaire? My thanks also to Genoclysm and Zephyros, both of whom helped me explore some of the more obscure aspects of Lore's history without ever asking why. Alina has done a stunning job of making this poor scribe look good. And, finally, for everyone who plays and dreams and creates for the sheer joy of it – for everyone who resides in Lore – home is where the heart is.

Foreword

Congratulations, everyone!!! The very first AdventureQuest novel has been published! This is an amazing accomplishment for our entire online community. On behalf of the team and players we would like to congratulate Lyra Trice Solis: loving mother of six, level 132 Necromancer in AdventureQuest (well, Lizardwoman scribe), admired fan-writer on the forums... and now published author of AdventureQuest: The Dragon's Secret.

Lyra Trice Solis' wild story is brimming with unexpected action, brand-new adventures, and memorable characters. It follows a young mage apprentice named John as he struggles to make his way in a world full of magic, mystery, and monsters. Along the way you will meet many new characters as well as some familiar faces from the games.

Our friendly team has been growing AdventureQuest and our other web-based games for 8 years. With over 101 million registered players, our crazy weekly releases are inspired by ideas, feedback, and stories from the amazing players (maybe you?) on our games' forums. This novel is the ultimate testament to the creative power of the community behind the games. We invite you to join us at http://forums2.battleon.com.

Battle On!

Artix, Galanoth & the entire BattleOn Games Team

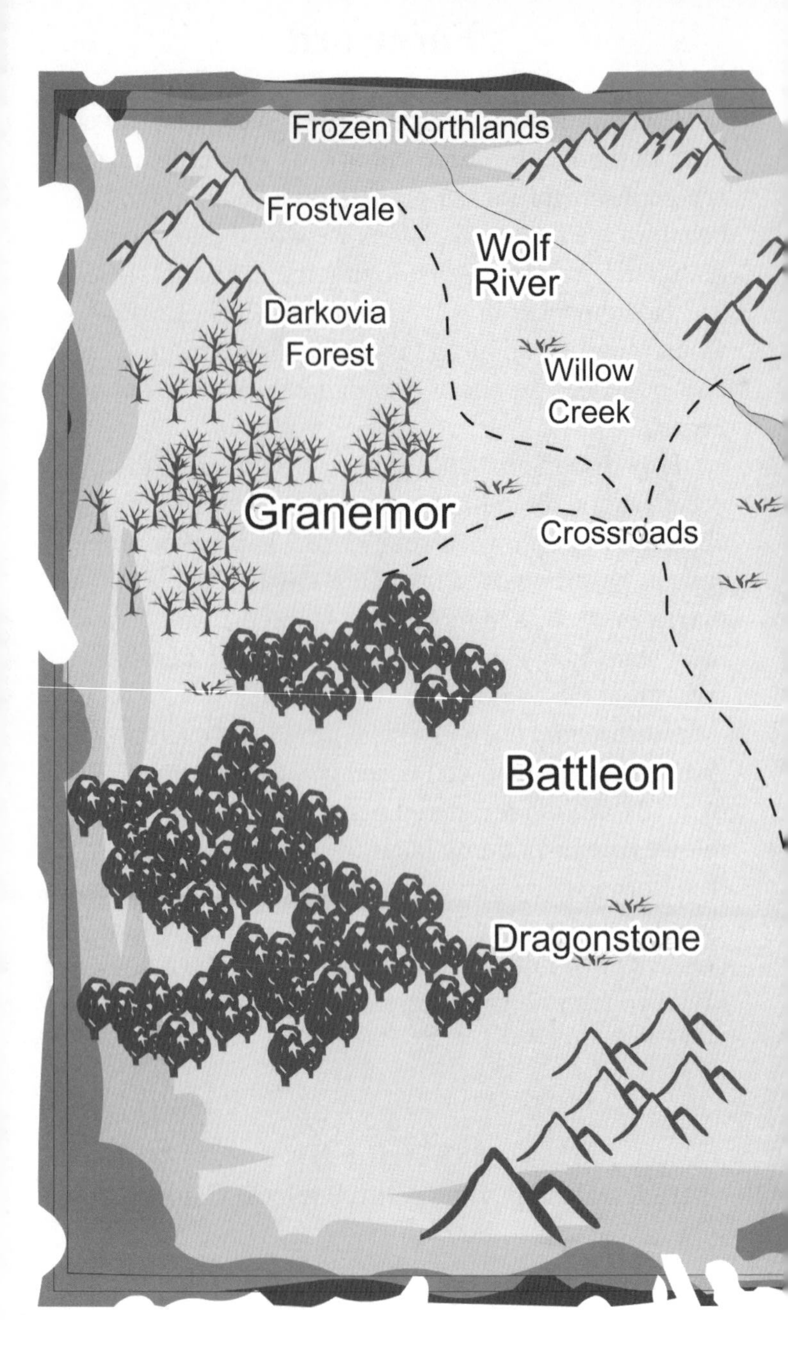
Frozen Northlands
Frostvale
Wolf River
Darkovia Forest
Willow Creek
Granemor
Crossroads
Battleon
Dragonstone

Dwarfhold Mts.
Ninjutsu Temple
Fairwind Spring
Dragonspine
Lolosia
Krovesport
Pirate's Cove
???
N
Skraeling Desert, Fire Fields, and Smoke Mt.

“I suppose I better take him on,” said the elderly mage. “Before he destroys half the countryside.”

Chapter One

The bully held John Black by the collar of his tunic, dangling him over the village well. "You bring it on yourself, Black," Krag said with a heavy sigh. "If you'd keep your mouth shut and learn some respect, I wouldn't have to do this to you, now, would I?"

"And if you weren't a tin-headed troll with ears the size of dinner plates, I wouldn't be forced to make fun of you. We both do what we've got to do, so you might as well get it over with, Krag."

It was predictable. It was the way things were. A couple of times a week, John would get dropped down the well or flung into the stinking mud of a pig pen, and Krag and all his followers would hoot with laughter and go on their way. Sooner or later someone would come by and extricate John from wherever he was stuck, and life would go on.

Until today.

Today, John had actually managed to attach a dinner plate to each side of a pig's head with a collar, and then had freed it to go squealing and running through the village wearing Krag's favorite tunic.

First Krag caught the pig, then he caught John.

Krag had marched John over to the big barn, and then tied him to the hay pulley with a fat rope. He hoisted John a couple of feet off the ground and then gave his leggings a good yank.

"Hey!" said John, trying to look down to see what was showing. "Krag, come on, this isn't right."

Smiling grimly, Krag had produced a tin of red paint and a paintbrush, and proceeded to paint a big red bulls-eye on John's butt. That done, he hoisted John up in the air some more, till he was high enough up that the whole village could see him dangling.

John thought Krag was done until Krag produced a dart blower.

"Oh, hey, no, Krag! Look, I'm sorry – ouch! – about the pig thing. I really – ouch! – am! It was more of a – ouch! – tribute than anything else! Really, Krag, I love you! Ouch! Ouch! Ouch!"

By now, a good portion of the village had gathered under the barn and were looking up at John's predicament and laughing.

There didn't seem to be much for John to do except hope that Krag ran out of darts really, really soon. On the plus side, it didn't seem like things could get any worse, either. Until his mother showed up with Ily, the pretty blond girl from the neighboring farm. John could feel his face getting as red as the bulls-eye on his backside.

Ily just stood there and gaped while John's mother squinted up at him. "John, get down from there right now!"

"Mom, I didn't actually get myself up here. I can't just get myself down!"

Recognizing the truth in that statement, John's mother looked around until she spotted Krag, who was still holding the dart gun. "Krag Miller! Get him down from there right now, before I go get your father!"

Obligingly, Krag reached for the fat pulley rope he'd tied off to a post.

"No! Mom! Krag!" John could already see what was going to happen.

Krag untied the rope, and it slithered around the post as John plummeted to the ground.

John closed his eyes and waited for the crash, but it didn't come. Instead, he felt a surge of … light? Can a person *feel* light? There was a gasp from the surrounding crowd.

Cautiously, John opened one eye.

He was floating about four feet off the ground. If he didn't know better, he'd swear that beams of light were shooting from his feet and keeping him up in the air. That surging feeling of power came back and he pushed at it with his mind, just a little. His body floated away from the direction of his push. There was another gasp from the crowd, and people scurried to get out of his way.

He pictured his feet, filled with light energy, swinging toward the ground. His body slowly became vertical. Grinning, he opened both eyes. Pushing the light energy out of his body, he repelled the rope that was now loosely coiled around him, raised his arms like a sorcerer, then pointed one hand at Krag.

"Krag, you are so gonna hurt for this one!"

Krag, his mouth hanging open, watched helplessly as power gathered at John's fingertips.

John pictured a ball of light shooting out of his hand and blasting Krag right in the gut.

The ball of light formed and flew out of his hand just like he pictured it. What John hadn't pictured was that the ball of light missed Krag and hit the ground while John flew backwards, landing on his tender bottom.

John pulled himself to his feet as Krag howled with laughter. Even Ily was laughing. Was that a smile on his mother's face?

Ignoring the draining feeling that came from using the power, John reached for the light and shoved *hard* at the ground. He soared into the air. He willed another ball of light into his open hand. This time he wouldn't screw it up! He pictured the ball of light flying from his fingertips and crashing into Krag's big, fat head until his flapping ears were all that was left.

There was a sizzle as the ball of light left John's fingers and missed again, hitting the side of the barn as John shot backwards like a rocket. He flew over the nearest hill and landed in the top of a cherrup tree. *Suns!* John thought as he struggled in the branches. If this was going to be a regular thing, he was going to have to work on his landings.

The discussion between John's father and mother

was very brief, and barely involved John at all.

"Maybe the mage in Hayfield would take him," said John's mother.

"What do you mean, 'take me'?" asked John.

"Probably for the best," replied John's father. "He gets in enough trouble *without* magic. Can you imagine what it would be like around here now that he has magic powers?"

"Sounds pretty good to me," said John. "We wouldn't have to herd the cows – I could fly 'em where they need to go."

Both parents stopped pacing to look at John, then at each other.

"I'll pack his things," said his mother.

"I'll go see if Doney can come over and help with the chores while we're gone," said John's father.

"Oh, come on. You're kidding, right? Doney?"

"You're right, John."

"Thank you!"

"I'll see if Krag can do it."

His mother and father didn't waste any time. The next day, they were all up at the crack of dawn. John's mother wrapped up a loaf of bread and some hard cheese while John's father helped him shove his spare clothes into a rucksack. With a kiss and a wave from John's mother, they set off to Hayfield. It was well into spring, but the morning air was cool, and John wore a sweater made by his mother over his tunic.

They walked in silence for a few minutes, then John said what was on his mind. "Dad, I can figure this out on my own. I don't want to leave home and go live with some geezer I don't even know. Not to mention he could turn me into a toad if he doesn't like me."

"John, we've already talked about this. If you have magic – real magic, not the ordinary, everyday, 'where did I put my walking-stick' kind of magic – you need to be trained by a real mage. I can't help you with that. And, seeing the trouble that you're able to get into *without* magic, I'm not sure being turned into a toad would be the worst thing that could happen to you."

John rubbed his butt, which was still sore. Maybe his dad had a point. Krag sure had.

Hefting his rucksack, John picked up his pace a little.

Qilder, the mage, lived in a cottage on the outskirts of the next village. It took them most of the afternoon to walk there and, when they arrived, their welcome was less than warm.

When John's father explained why they were there, the old man had glowered at John under thick white eyebrows. "He doesn't look very magical to me," the mage had growled.

John looked uncertainly at his father, who made an encouraging motion with his hand. "Show him, John. Show him what you did at the barn."

John took a deep breath and pictured light rushing down his arm and into his hand, forming it into a flashing ball.

The old mage's eyebrows rose. "Not bad."

"You haven't seen anything yet," said John's father. "Go ahead, John, let him see what you can do."

Closing his eyes, John pictured himself floating through the air and launched the ball at the ground. As it had before, the force of the light ball hitting the ground propelled John up into the air like a cork from a bottle. He opened his eyes with satisfaction as he soared up … up … up.

Then he started to come down … down … down.

Frantically, John formed and shot off another ball of light, which slowed his descent slightly. It also set the roof of the cottage alight.

He tried picturing the light flowing into his feet, but was too panicked to do a good job. The ground was getting dangerously close, dangerously fast. John threw another light ball and changed course again. Below him, John glimpsed his father and Qilder diving under the porch for cover.

With a heavy crash, John landed on the hen house, which promptly collapsed.

The hens set up a deafening screeching, and the rooster, with splinters of wood in his comb from the demolished coop, rushed over and pecked John on the top of the head.

"Hey! Ouch! Quit," shouted John, hastily scrambling to his feet and away from the indignant rooster.

His father and Qilder emerged from under the porch, and the mage waved a hasty hand to put out the fire on his roof. Qilder turned to survey his destroyed hen house.

He opened his mouth to speak, and John and his father both cringed. John was pretty sure he was going to be turned into something unpleasant on the spot.

But the elderly mage just sighed. "I suppose I better take him on," Qilder said. "Before he destroys half the countryside."

The sudden appearance of John's magical abilities was not unique, Qilder explained over tea. It had probably always been there in a latent form, requiring an event sufficiently scary – or in John's case, humiliating – to bring it to the fore, he said. Most people were born with theirs and, as they grew older, their magic slowly grew stronger. Actually, Qilder said, it was likely that most everyone had some latent magical ability, a potential that simply went untapped in the vast majority of people because they never had the motivation to use or develop it. John's case wasn't unheard of, but he had some catching up to do in order to be able to understand and control his abilities. At the moment, they were a bit of a wild card.

"I don't understand why I have to practice all the time," John said in frustration after a particularly tedious magic lesson. "Especially all this stupid *little* stuff."

"First of all," said Qilder, in a mildly offended tone, "no magic is *little* magic, apprentice. Secondly, if you master the small things, the large things will fall into place naturally. Wild magic, which is what you have, is just that. Wild. You have plenty of wild magic. What you do not have is control. When you develop control over the small things, such as producing a steady light at your fingertips, you will find that the bigger things, such as using your light to propel you through the air, will be within your grasp."

John sighed and went back to trying to form a small, steady ball of light that he could move between his fingers at will. Once he had mastered that, Qilder informed him, his next task would be to learn to pass the ball of light from hand to hand, and then from hand to object to hand, all without the ball losing its shape or consistency.

While Qilder was not as impressed as John by John's ability to fling himself short distances through the air by pushing off solid objects with a burst of light, he didn't stop his young apprentice from fiddling with it – as long as his chores were done first.

Fortunately for John, Qilder kept a good supply of healing balm on hand.

Other than his disagreement with Qilder on what the direction of his lessons should be, John and his elderly master got on well together. They settled into a comfortable routine. Qilder was up at the crack of dawn and expected John to be too, drawing water for the porridge, collecting a couple of eggs from the nice fat hens that Qilder kept, then settling into a companionable breakfast before starting lessons. The first lesson of John's day was learning to read – two hours of that, then a lunch of bread and cheese before magic practice started. Learning to read had been the other thing they frequently disagreed about.

Qilder had been horrified when he found out John couldn't read. It was the only thing that John had really seen Qilder get worked up about since they'd met.

"I can't understand it," Qilder would say, shaking his head as John laboriously traced out his letters on a piece of parchment paper. "How can a boy even consider being a mage without knowing how to read and write? How can you look up spells and read the magical tomes in the wizard's libraries if you can't read?"

"I didn't know I was going to be a mage until a few weeks ago," John would explain. "I hadn't exactly planned on this as a career. Besides, I'm going to be a mage. I'll just conjure up whatever I need. What has reading got to do with it?"

That usually got him a *thunk* on the back of the head.

"Only a fool would put great power in the hands of an ignoramus," Qilder would reply. "And I'm no fool. If you want to learn from me, you'll have to demonstrate you deserve what I can teach you."

And once again, he would instruct John to copy whatever text Qilder had set before him, often at mind-numbing length. Then he'd correct John's letters and order them re-written.

"You'd best learn fast now, apprentice. You've got a lot of catching up to do."

Once a week, Qilder declared a day of no lessons – magical or otherwise. They would spend their time doing the homely chores that needed to be done to keep body and soul together – mending the pasture fences where the goats and the milk cow were kept, tending the vegetable garden, making the soaps or potions or balms that the local villagers favored. They would go to the market to barter for whatever they couldn't make on their own and, in the evening, Qilder would buy him a hot pie at the local tavern and let John wander the town while he settled in for a good gossip.

It was during one such session that John first heard about the dragon ravaging the countryside to the south and east of their own village.

John had eaten his pie – blackberry sweetened with honey, wrapped in a fried crust that was hot enough to burn his fingers – then wandered the village, joining some of the other boys in a game of hoops and lingering at the local well for a drink of cool water and a look at the girls who came to fill their buckets there.

When the air had begun to dim and cool he had gone back to the tavern to seek his master.

Qilder was sitting at a table with several other men, a dark look on his face. John came over and sat on the floor at Qilder's feet, leaning back against the stone wall behind him. Qilder had showed John how to generate a small but powerful light at his fingertips, and they often stayed late at the tavern during their weekly excursions, trusting John's magic to see them safely home, moons or no.

This night the tavern didn't have its usual rollicking atmosphere – there was no fiddler, no table full of raucous gamblers, no one inspired by too many cups of hard cider to try to dance a jig. Even the two hounds that belonged to the owner were quiet, lying listlessly by the hearth, instead of making their rounds doing tricks for tidbits of the patrons' food.

The tavern was as solemn as a grave.

Knowing better than to demand information, John sat quietly and listened to the low-voiced conversation taking place at Qilder's table.

"Aye, 'tis the third village, I've heard, in as many weeks."

"The dragon has run amuck! I heard that Galanoth the dragon slayer has been sent for."

"That won't bring back those it already roasted."

"'Tis a fire dragon, then?"

"Some say it's more than just one dragon."

"I hear that there's a whole army of them fire dragons – and the one as leads them is mad as a snowman in summer."

John shivered, half scared, half thrilled by the story. He dozed as the conversation went on, dreaming of flying high up into the air using his light power, tossing massive beams of light at the foul dragons that winged and circled around him until each and every one had been felled and he landed in a field full of cheering villagers. Then Ily would run forward to press delighted kisses all over his face.

"John, John," she said, voice hoarse with gratitude.

"It wasn't that much," said John modestly.

"John!" Ily replied, much more forcefully. For no reason, she burst out laughing, then hit his leg with a stick.

John's eyes popped open to see one of the dogs standing right in front of him, lapping happily at the pie crumbs on John's face. He realized it was Qilder's voice he had heard calling his name, Qilder's staff that he had been tapped with.

And he saw, looking around, the rest of the tavern's occupants that had been laughing. *Suns!* He must have been talking in his sleep or something.

Stiffly, he got to his feet. "I'm glad I could lighten up the atmosphere in here a little."

Qilder waved a hand. "Time to take your old master home, John. Make us a light, will you?"

John let the light surge down into his fingertips and burst out in a bright glow that lit every dim corner of the tavern. There was a collective "ahh" of appreciation from the other patrons that did a lot to soothe John's embarrassment at mistaking some stupid old hound for Ily. Qilder's lips curved up, and John realized the old man had planned it that way. A rush of love for the elderly mage filled John and he grinned, good spirits restored. "If you are too tired to walk, master," John said loudly, "I could fly you home."

Qilder's eyes narrowed. John had attempted to fly again many times since coming to Qilder's. Each attempt had met with some kind of disaster – usually revolving around the landing. Whatever Qilder was thinking, though, it didn't show on his face. "That's all right, young apprentice. It's too few steps to waste your magic on, really. And I'd like to stretch these old bones for a minute. Helps me sleep. Let's go home the conventional way – on our feet."

It wasn't until hours later that John remembered the conversation about the dragon that had destroyed three villages.

The next week, on chore day, Qilder sent John out to the surrounding hills to gather early leaves from the *sanare* plants that grow on the rocky slopes. Later Qilder would use them to make a healing balm that was highly prized by the neighboring villagers.

Having gathered a small basket full of the leaves, careful to follow Qilder's instructions not to strip any single plant in his gathering, John climbed to the top of the hill and lay back on a sun-warmed rock, blasting small, fluffy clouds until it occurred to him that farmers hoping for rain might not like that. Feeling slightly guilty, John decided to try to create clouds instead, focusing on the great blue sky over his head and trying to visualize clouds into existence.

After a few minutes, John was surprised and pleased to see several big, white clouds blowing across his line of sight. Then he got a whiff of something … odd. Unsettling. It smelled like smoke. But why would he be smelling smoke way out here by himself? There were no cottages except for Qilder's for quite a distance, and even Qilder's cottage was too far for his little fire to be carried along the breeze.

Uneasy, John sat up and looked around him. The hilltop he had chosen to rest on gave him a bird's eye view of the surrounding area. He noticed one thing right away.

Those weren't clouds that had been rolling across

the sky.

They were plumes of smoke.

Below, Qilder's cottage was a smoldering ruin. In the distance, John could see other plumes of smoke rising from the village where Qilder plied his trade. And even further, off to the west, more smoke roiled. John's gut tightened. Qilder's village wasn't the only village burning that day. Unless John was seriously mistaken, his parents' village was burning as well. Above it, a red dragon circled once and then flew off into the distance.

In a state of shock, John slammed down the hillside, using his unreliable magic as best he could to hurry himself forward, skidding through small rock falls and skinning up hands and knees in his haste to get to Qilder's cottage.

Or what remained of it.

When he arrived, his throat was raw from the sickening smoke that filled the air. It was no longer a billowing, cloud-like white, but a grimy yellow, and reeked of brimstone and the unthinkable things that fueled the fire that birthed it.

John screamed Qilder's name, but nothing stirred. In the little chicken coop, all that was left of Qilder's plump hens were small charred lumps on the ground.

The cottage itself was a smoldering heap. The fire had burned away the peat roof, then the timbers that had supported it. A hot wind flew up, full of ash and spark.

He knew that in there somewhere, buried beneath the embers, beneath the shattered timbers, lay Qilder. Tears as hot as the embers burned his eyes.

At the edge of John's vision, he caught a flicker of motion and whirled, one hand raised, a ball of light ready to blast the dragon he expected to see. Hoped to see. At that moment, with the ruins of Qilder's neat little cottage all around him and everything it had contained turned into char, there was nothing John wanted more than to die taking out the dragon who had done this. The desire seared his chest with a bitter heat.

A huge man in dark armor stepped forward, visor pushed up so that John could see his quick eyes taking in the scene. The visor was shaped like the skull of a dragon, complete with jagged sharp teeth, and covered with a dark metal that made the dragon's snarl look incredibly sinister. A ragged scarlet cape fluttered behind him. He carried a sword as long as John was tall, broad as the trunk of a tree. Planting the point of the mighty sword in front of him, he leaned on the hilt as he turned his eyes toward John.

"This was your home?"

John nodded, not sure he could squeeze words past the fists of grief and rage that gripped his throat.

"And you were off somewhere when it happened. Saw it?"

Again, John nodded.

"A large dragon, red as fire?"

Before John could nod again, a strange prickling sensation ran up his back, and he jerked his eyes to the sky just in time to scream out a warning.

The huge man whirled, blade coming up, and the

dragon veered off. John could hear a horrible chortling sound coming from it as it flew out of the warrior's reach.

A single word was ground out from the man's clenched jaw. "Akriloth!"

The dragon hissed, and flame shot from his snout. "Galanoth. Head of the Dragon Slayers. You move swiftly. Give me the boy and I will let you crawl away. This time."

The dragon slayer moved between John and the wheeling dragon. "I will sacrifice no one to you, Akriloth, now or ever. Come within reach of my blade, and we will settle this now."

Akriloth laughed again, that horrible hissing sound that made John's teeth ache. The dragon swooped low, and without thought, John dived out from behind the dragon slayer and threw a ball of light at the dragon, who wobbled slightly in his path and then soared back up higher into the air. The dragon angled his flight and eyed John narrowly, then suddenly dove, a clawed foot reaching for the young mage.

The dragon was quick, but Galanoth was quicker. Even as John screamed defiance and stood straight, daring the dragon to take him, Galanoth dived between the two and blocked the dragon's fiery breath with his cloak. The dragon's claws grabbed the dragon slayer instead of John. Flipping his blade around as lightly as if it were made of paper, Galanoth struck a mighty blow across the dragon's scaled leg. The dragon emitted a high-pitched screech and dropped the dragon slayer to the ground. Akriloth circled them twice from high overhead, blood sizzling as it fell through the air, then shot off across the sky and disappeared in the distance.

John watched until Akriloth disappeared, then turned to Galanoth, who had the same intense look on his face that John could feel stretched across his own. He knew that if Galanoth could have flown after the dragon, he would have. Walking over, John looked at Galanoth's cape.

"Fire-proof?"

"My mother was an enchantress. It was her last gift to me."

"That armor as heavy as it looks?" At first it had looked like the thick dull grey of iron, but now that he was closer, John could see that the metal looked almost … alive, somehow, strange runes chasing themselves across a surface that was as dark as night one second, a starlit silver the next.

This time Galanoth laughed.

"Hardly. The dragon's teeth weigh more than the armor proper." He gestured at the sinister spikes thrusting up from the pauldrons covering his shoulders, and John realized the spikes were indeed dragon's teeth, covered in the same strange metal that made up the rest of the armor.

He angled his head up, looking the dragon slayer in the eye.

"Have you been to the villages?" asked John, hate for Akriloth loosening his throat. "I didn't realize that it was smoke, not clouds, crossing the sky until I got high enough up to see."

"I've been to the farther village. I came from the west, down the mountainside, where I could see the trail of smoke for many miles. Followed it to its source, then the dragon himself this way. Always a step behind, curse him." Galanoth's eyes narrowed. "But he won't be able to avoid me forever."

"Are … are the people in the farther village dead?"

Galanoth turned sympathetic eyes to John. "Is that where you are from?"

Throat tight again, John nodded. "I had just apprenticed here, to the mage Qilder." All dead. Qilder, his parents, Ily, even Krag.

Galanoth reached out a hand to John's shoulder. "I'm sorry. I know how hard this must be for you."

"Do you?"

Galanoth nodded. "My own family died in a dragon attack, years ago. I founded the Order of Dragon Slayers and dedicated myself to wiping the black-hearted devils from the face of Lore forever."

John felt a small trickle of warmth. The dragon slayer wasn't just saying that. He really did understand.

Galanoth whistled and a huge warhorse appeared. "I need to search through the village and see if there are any survivors. He has left none so far, but there is always a chance. Have you the stomach for that?"

John squared his shoulders, and looked at Galanoth with steady eyes. "I do."

"Good. After we're done, I can give you a ride to the next village if you like, but after that I must be off in pursuit of Akriloth before he kills again."

John looked at the scorched ground around them. There was nothing left for him to pack and take with him. Galanoth swung himself up and into the broad leather saddle and sheathed his blade. Reaching down, he held out a hand to John.

Taking one last look around, John scrambled onto the horse behind the dragon slayer. He kept his eyes focused on the sky as they rode off.

Just in case.

Chapter Two

True to his word, after Galanoth finished the grisly search for survivors, he gave John a ride to the next village. While he was there, Galanoth met with the village elders to discuss the recent dragon activity.

Understandably, the elders were quite alarmed to learn about other villages in the area being attacked and destroyed by the dragon Akriloth.

"I don't understand," said Councilor Sprizz, an old man with a querulous voice. "Why have we heard nothing of this? Respectfully, great dragon slayer, why have you not slain the dragon already? You're galumphing all over the countryside one step behind him while he rains destruction down on everyone in his path. Will you wait until he kills us all and then swoop in to save the day? Because if we're all dead of dragon fire when it happens, there won't be much of a parade in your honor."

Galanoth flushed, but he met the old man's challenging gaze head on. Without his helmet, Galanoth looked younger than John had thought. His face was noble, befitting a knight, and he was as fearless when being berated by the old man as he had been when he threw himself between John and the attacking dragon.

"Akriloth is crafty beyond measure, Councilman Sprizz. He has destroyed each village so completely that there was no one left to tell the tale. What came to me was a distant rumor of destruction brought by a traveling healer who had sought a village and found only char. I found the second and third villages while attempting to find the first, and the trail there was cold as a stone. When I saw the trail of smoke reaching up to the sky, I raced to get there, but was in time to find only the cooling embers of my companion's home village."

Galanoth put a hand on John's shoulder and, for an uncomfortable minute, all eyes were on him.

"John Black's parents, friends, and neighbors are all dead of dragon fire. I searched the wreckage myself for survivors and found nothing but the dead shells of the people who once lived there. As I prepared to leave, I saw yet another plume of fire-smoke on the horizon, and followed it to the home of John's master, Mage Qilder. John had been out searching for ingredients for his master's healing balm when the dragon struck. He is the only survivor out of five villages that I have been able to find, and we were attacked ourselves by Akriloth, the fire dragon who is responsible for these vicious attacks."

"Yet *you* survived," said Sprizz, but his voice was quieter now, as if the recounting of the horrific devastation that Galanoth had witnessed took some of the steam from his kettle.

"We survived, Councilman Sprizz, because facing an armed and ready dragon slayer is a quite a different matter from attacking unarmed and unprepared farmers." Galanoth's voice was hard as iron, cold as ice. A shiver of awe ran up John's back as he listened.

"And now," continued Galanoth, "we have identified Akriloth as the murderer. I go in search of him in his lair, rather than waiting for him to come forth and kill again. I ask one boon of you before I go."

"And what is that, dragon slayer? Weapons? A fresh horse? Provisions for your journey? Whatever we may do to succor you on your hunt, we shall gladly do." It was another councilor, speaking warmly as if to make up for the other man's skeptical attitude.

Galanoth smiled and suddenly looked nearly as young as John. "Thank you for your kindness, but I am well equipped for the task at hand. I ask only that you offer my companion a place to stay and food for his belly until he has had a chance to recover from the horrors he has witnessed and choose his own path."

"Wait," said John, panicked. "I want to go with you! He killed my family! Surely, you mean for me to go with you – I'm a mage, I can help. I won't get in your way, I eat hardly anything!" John heard the pleading note in his own voice, but he didn't care. All he wanted was revenge on Akriloth – or if he could not kill the dragon himself, to die making it possible for another to do so.

Galanoth turned kind eyes on John. "A great mage you will be some day, John Black, I have no doubt. But you have survived an experience that would paralyze many a full-fledged warrior with terror. Few talk with the dragon and live. It is my task to avenge these grievous wrongs. I am the Dragon Slayer. It is your task to stay here and protect this village if needed, and to let your heart heal so you can get on with the job of becoming the man you are destined to be."

"But, but–"

Again, Galanoth placed his hand on John's shoulder. "This is my word, and my word is my bond. I will not take you to face death in the claws of a dragon for a second time. You will remain here and carry on the name of your father and the memory of your mother. Keep alive the tale of the evil done here by the dragon Akriloth so that all know the evil that lurks in the hearts of dragon-kind and understand why they must be destroyed – every last black-hearted one – down the last shard of the last cursed egg."

No matter how John protested, he was unable to change Galanoth's mind, and it was with a heavy heart that he watched the dragon slayer ride from the village on his huge war horse. Galanoth turned to give John a wave, which the younger man returned dispiritedly. He understood Galanoth's reasoning, but John was truly lost now; sorrow and grief and exhaustion fed on his heart with sharp teeth.

John felt a stirring at his side and turned. It was the old councilor, Sprizz. The one who had been so critical of Galanoth. He was eying John with interest, and there was a glint in his eye that made John distinctly uneasy.

"So, you're a mage, eh? You may stay with me. I

am sure we will find some use for you."

All John wanted to do was find a place to lie down and sleep for about a thousand years. And then, hopefully, wake up and find out this had all been some kind of horrible nightmare. He started to protest, then shrugged. What difference did it make? What difference did any of it make when, in a moment of dragon's fire, a person's entire life could be changed forever, and everything you loved and cared about could be snatched away like a child's candy? With heavy steps, he walked after the councilor.

That summer, John felt as if he moved through a field of hip-deep mud. While Councilman Sprizz wanted much from John, he gave little in return.

For several weeks it had been, "young mage, this," and "sir mage, that," until Sprizz had finally realized that there was very little John could do magically that could actually benefit the councilor.

When Sprizz found out the limits of John's uncertain magic, he had been furious. "You were presented to us as a mage!" he shrieked, spittle flying from his lips. "All you can do is fling yourself through the hills like a doll tossed by an angry child and make a night light with your fingers. Bah! You will have to do more than that to earn your keep around here, you wretched orphan!"

And so it was. John's new place to sleep was in

the barn on a pile of hay, with just a thin horse blanket for covering on a chilly night. His food was … well, it wouldn't have surprised him if his meals were culled from what Councilman Sprizz fed the pigs, and Councilman Sprizz did not care overmuch for his pigs. It was up to John to muck out the stalls, haul the water, repair the fences and plow the fields. It was John who dug the new cistern and repaired the roof and shod the horses, and it was John who harvested the early summer crops and hauled them to the market.

One day, he was stopped there by Janne, the daughter of a neighboring farmer. "Why do you do this, Mage John?"

He looked at her dully. It had been months since anyone had spoken to him without anger in their voice, without yet another demand for work. "Do what, Janne?" His voice was hoarse. How long had it been since he had actually spoken with someone?

"My father said that when you came to town with the dragon slayer, he said that one day you would be a great mage. But you stay here and slop the pigs and work like a slave for Councilman Sprizz, and he treats you worse than a beast in the field. Why do you allow it?"

John looked at her blankly. He couldn't think of an answer to that to save his life. Why was he living like this? He thought of the trouble Mage Qilder had done to teach him his letters, his assurances that if John worked hard, he would grow into his magic.

Janne waited patiently for an answer, as ideas tumbled in John's brain. He felt a great wash of shame that he had been reduced to such a mind-numbed state that he had turned his back on everything his parents had hoped for him, that Qilder had worked for with him, that Galanoth had thought him capable of. Then he shrugged, and moved past her without answering. Any answer he could give would sound so stupid it wasn't worth the effort of opening his mouth.

But the words she had spoken wouldn't let go of his brain.

That night he lay on a bed of hay, prickly strands poking through the tattered blanket he had thrown down underneath himself. Janne's words echoed in his head. "Why do you do this, Mage John?"

He was exhausted, and needed to sleep. He turned on his side, and her words sounded in his ears. "Why do you do this, Mage John?"

He flipped over to the other side. "Why do you do this, Mage John?"

John sat up in the dark and yelled at the top of his lungs, "I don't know! But I'm not going to do it anymore!"

In the house, a dog barked and a light went on. The councilman's sleep had been disturbed.

Feeling better, John lay back down and went to sleep.

In the days that followed, a series of inexplicable events transpired on Councilman Sprizz's property. His private well dried up, and when he sent John to fetch water at the village's communal well, all the buckets sprung leaks. The chimney became blocked with soot between one day and the next, filling the house with pungent smoke and sending its occupants choking and coughing into the yard. The leather straps that held Councilman Sprizz's mattress to his bed frame came loose, and when the councilman lay down one night, he found himself unceremoniously dumped on the floor. The rooster developed a habit of perching right beneath the councilman's bedroom window and crowing – in the middle of the night. The milk soured three days running before it made the trip from goat to pail. And someone snuck into the pasture one night and painted an accurate, if unflattering, portrait of Councilman Sprizz on the rump of each one of his prized heifers.

The councilman was fit to be tied, and it wasn't long before his suspicions fell on apprentice mage John Black.

When a handful of sourberries were found inside John's milking pail, the councilman's rage spilled out of control.

"You wretched, ungrateful … *orphan*!" He spluttered, as if *orphan* were some kind of insult. "I should have known it was you all along, you devil's imp! You'll go straight to the … straight to the … straight to the magistrate?" Councilman Sprizz lost steam as he watched John play with a small ball of light, rolling it across his fingertips, around the back of his hand, then bouncing it from palm to palm, all the while apparently listening with silent respect.

When the councilman's yelling had petered out, John looked up politely to see if he was done.

"Have you ever seen what one of these babies can do to field full of corn?" asked John, in a conversational tone. "I bet not. Or how it can scatter a herd of cows when a globe of light explodes in front of them? They'll run for miles. It's quite a sight to see. Of course, someone needs to go gather them up eventually, which is a lot of work, but still, it's pretty entertaining."

"You wouldn't dare!" said the councilman, but his voice wasn't as certain as his words.

"Me?" said John, as if he were surprised. "Why would I do something like that to the man who has been like a father to me?"

"Indeed," said the councilman, but it came out in something suspiciously like a squeak.

"Anyway," said John, "it's not as if I lie awake every night practicing and thinking of ways to take vengeance on those who have abused me or taken advantage of me. Besides, who would be stupid enough to take advantage of a mage whose powers could someday completely ruin them? Only a fool would do that. And we both know that you are anything but a fool, Councilman Sprizz."

The councilor watched John bouncing the ball of light between his palm and the floor, and turned a satisfying shade of green.

"All those things being true, though, councilman, I feel it's time for me to take my leave and strike out on my own. A man can only live on the charity of others for so long, don't you agree?"

Gulping, the councilman nodded. "Perhaps I could help provision you for your trip, John."

John smiled. "That would be very kind of you,

Councilman Sprizz."

John set off with a new rucksack stuffed with a blanket, a change of clothes, dried apples, cheese, and bread. He had new boots, a knife in his pocket, flint and tinder, and a hearty staff for walking with.

On his way out of the village, he stopped to say goodbye to Janne.

"I wanted to say thanks," he blurted, while her mother watched them carefully from the porch.

"For what, John Black?" He'd never seen hair as pretty as hers, or eyes as blue. She looked at him questioningly.

"For … for waking me up, I guess. You made me realize that I was just coasting along, and that this is not what my parents or Galanoth would have wanted for me."

She smiled at him, and he suddenly felt at least a foot taller.

"Take good care of yourself on the road, now, mage."

"You too, Janne. Take good care of yourself."

"Maybe someday, when you are a famous mage, you will come back and visit our small village again."

"Not on your li—" looking at her, it suddenly occurred to him that maybe there was at least one good reason to think about returning some day. "I mean, probably. Probably some day I will be back."

"That would be good, then, Mage John. I will look for you, someday." And, darting a glance at her observant mother, she pressed a quick kiss to his cheek and fled back into the house in a whirl of skirts.

With a new spring in his step, John Black headed out toward his future.

Being on the road was not as easy as it looked, John learned. He spent many nights sleeping out in the open, and more than a few wondering where his next meal was coming from. Despite his show for Councilman Sprizz, his control over his magic had shown less improvement than he would have liked, and there were only so many ways a young man could make a living as a human lantern.

Plus, there were other vagabonds and rogues to watch out for. More than once, John had happened upon a group of miscreants who thought having a young servant to fetch and carry – and break into the occasional farmhouse – would be just the thing. He'd had a couple of narrow escapes before he had learned proper caution.

Once, he had been able to use the power of his light magic to foil a midnight robbery attempt. But it had been as much surprise that sent the robbers scurrying as anything else; if they had stayed and fought, he would have been lost.

The miller he had saved from robbery had been effusively grateful and had given John a small pouch of gold coins, but that had only lasted for a short time, no matter how he tried to stretch it.

Still, being on the road wasn't all bad. He had continued to practice his letters, and had spent one of his precious gold coins at a book-vendor's stall in a village market. The youth who ran the stall was tall and thin to the point of emaciation, unkempt white hair almost covering eyes that didn't seem quite focused on the here-and-now. After careful consideration, John settled on a battered book, *A Brief History of Magic*, by Stefen Hawks.

He began using the book to practice his reading until it felt like his eyes were bleeding. He practiced writing his words with a stick he had carved down to a stylus point, writing in the dirt or tracing the fine script in his *History*.

It was awhile before he was able to make enough sense of the words on the page to start thinking about their *meaning*.

He had sounded out all the words in the section on staffs, for example, several times before it occurred to him that something in there might apply to the staff that he was using, day in and day out, to range the countryside. After several tries, John thought he had the knack of directing his light magic down the long, wooden shaft and out the tip, which saved his fingertips being seared by a bolt of light gone wrong. It also proved pretty hard on the staffs, and he went through several before he read farther and determined that he needed a focal point on the end of the staff to truly focus the power of the light he sent coursing through it.

John learned that the best focal point for a fully

working staff was a seed-pod of an almost-extinct crystal tree, mounted to his staff with incantations and magical scribings. Not only did he have no idea where almost extinct crystal trees lurked at, he was still learning to scribe plain old Lorian, much less magical runes and commands.

A light stone was more common and could also do the trick, but he didn't know where to find one of those, either.

As John read and thought, he also rambled the countryside, and one day found himself on the banks of a wide river. He followed its path until he came to a cluster of cottages where a family of boatmen made their living carrying people to and fro across the river.

"The Wolf River, it is," one of the ferrymen explained. "Runs all the way from the Frozen Northlands to the bay what Krovesport is stuck onto."

"How much does it cost to get across?" asked John.

The boatman named a figure that might as well have been a thousand gold coins, as John had no money left. "That's for going by yourself," he explained. "We have a ferry boat that can be shared by many, but it only goes across twice a day. Brand new, she is, too," finished the boatman proudly.

"Have you a lot of need for a ferry boat that can carry so many?" said John.

"Oh, aye, with so many fleeing the dragon war, we do. 'Tis why we built her," said the man, as if John was a little slow.

"Dragon war? What is this?"

The man shook his head. "It's mostly south of here. The great red fire monster, Akriloth, has joined together all manner of fire creatures, and they rampage through the villages killing all they come across. The only thing holding them back from firin' the whole land is the hero Galanoth and his band of Dragon Slayers."

The name Akriloth sent a thrill of hatred through John. He lived still? And Galanoth still battled him?

The sudden rage that came over John turned his vision red and made the boatman take a step backward.

"Are you all right then, young traveler? Will you be needin' a boat after all?"

John forced himself to speak calmly. "I need to get to where the fighting is. Do you know where Galanoth and his men do battle against the great dragon?"

The boatman nodded. "Aye, I hear 'tis down at Smoke Mountain, where the dragon slayers have Akriloth and his army pinned."

"What's the best way to get there?"

The boatman thought for a moment, then spit on the ground. "Smoke Mountain lies that way," he said, pointing south. "But the shortest way ain't always the quickest way, if you follow me."

John, who had been ready to stride off at that second, turned and looked at the boatman. "What do you mean?"

The boatman shrugged. "That way's over mountains and across the Skraeling Desert is what I mean. A smart man would head to Krovesport and catch berth on a ship along the coast and through the Straits of Deridak. Then it's just a short cut overland to Smoke Mountain."

John nodded. "And to get to Krovesport?"

"Cross the river and then follow it on down to the bay, young sir. You'll get there soon enough."

The tricky part, John soon realized, was getting across Wolf River.

It was late summer, and it was already beginning to snow at the river's head. The water was freezing and much too cold to swim across. For that very reason, John hesitated to trust his light magic to thrust him across. If something went wrong – and it usually did – he'd end up dunked in the icy river, and no better off than if he'd decided to swim for it.

After sleeping on it, John decided to steal a boat and paddle across. He hated stealing on principle, but felt that his purpose was urgent enough to excuse a little petty larceny.

He spent most of a day scouting the banks of the river, looking for a boat small enough – and decrepit enough – that it was unlikely to be missed. He came across a goldenrod tree during his search for a boat, and found a thick branch to carve into a new staff, so it didn't feel like a total waste of time.

Finally, he found a small skiff, cached in a stand of cattails, and decided to give it a try. It was leaky as a sieve, he discovered, shortly after casting off the bank, and the one paddle it contained made hard work of any progress across the swift river. John paddled until his muscles screamed with exhaustion, and he was still only halfway across. Desperate, he looked downstream, where the river widened to meet the bay. He needed to get across *now*. The further he drifted, the greater the remaining distance across the river would be.

An idea came to him. Could he use light against the surface of the water the way he did against the earth on dry land? As a new leak sprang, he decided it was worth a try. Closing his eyes, he focused on the feeling of power streaking down his arm and forming a ball of light in his hand. He opened his eyes and flung the light like a stone from the back of the skiff. Just as he had hoped, the light went skipping across the deep water, and the skiff shot forward. John crowed with delight and made ready to skip another ball of light.

It was the work of just a few minutes for John to reach the opposite shore and pull the skiff securely up onto the bank.

For a moment, John considered the possibility of setting it adrift, then chasing it back across the river and up the bank by virtue of his light magic.

As he stood looking out over the river, a dead fish bobbed to the surface at his feet. Then another and another.

Aghast, he realized that the fish were all pointing directly at the skiff. In a panic, he picked up the little boat's single oar and tried to push the fish back under the water.

It didn't work. Looking up, he saw that the path of dead fish extended halfway across the river, to the exact spot that his first ball of light had faded out. Obviously, light magic didn't agree with the fish in Wolf River.

He looked around, guilty, to see if anyone had witnessed his murder of so many hapless fish. Seeing no one, he scrambled hastily up the bank and on his way before anyone could place him at the scene of the crime.

Qilder had been right. He still had a lot to learn.

After John made it across the river, getting to Krovesport was easy. There was a broad road that followed the river, with enough people on it that one more teenage boy didn't get much notice. A man on horseback came by, spreading a story about a mysterious river monster that shot lightning from its fins and killed fish for sport, but John kept his head down and his mouth shut and was careful not to shine a light where it could be seen by anyone else, so no one ever guessed the truth.

Once in Krovesport, John gravitated down toward the docks and discovered that a ship left for Dunderweed, the main port of Deridak Bay, every couple of weeks. It was not finding a ship that was the problem. It was finding a way *onto* the ship.

Finding passage was not the only thing that was proving difficult in Krovesport. There were no groves of fruit trees or vegetable gardens to help himself to, nor barns to find a pile of hay to rest on. Instead, John found himself reduced to theft for an apple or a piece of bread, and breaking into buildings to find a safe place to sleep, away from the ruffians and the gangs that roved the port late at night.

He'd been in town for about a week when he made a stealthy grab for a fat wallet that dangled from the belt of a local merchant. His plan had been to get in close and snick the man's purse strings with his knife, then catch the falling purse and get away before the man knew what had happened. Naive about the lengths to which the good citizens of Krovesport would go to in order to protect themselves, he hadn't seen the merchant's body guard, and when he found himself snatched up in the air and swinging by his collar from a fist the size of a ham, John's first thought was that Krag had survived the dragon attack and had followed John all the way to Krovesport.

"Ah ha!" said the merchant with satisfaction, squinting into John's face. "What kind of scrawny vagrant have we caught this time, Tombo?"

The burly bodyguard shrugged and looked pleased.

"Whatever we have caught, the magistrate will take care of him right enough, eh?"

The bodyguard nodded and gave John a little shake as he dangled the young man in the air.

"Oh, please, sir, please don't take me to the magistrate! I'll do anything – I'm a mage, sir, and could do wondrous magic on your behalf!"

The merchant burst out laughing. Even the bodyguard grinned.

From the rapidly gathering crowd of gawkers, someone called out, "That's no mage, I seen him beggin' outside the *Rusty Dagger* just two days ago!"

"And why would a mage be going around begging and stealing rich men's purses, eh, boy?" asked the merchant. He snapped his fingers under John's nose.

"That's for you and your magic."

Spotting a constable trying to thread his way through the gathered crowd, the merchant waved his fat hands. "You! Come and take this thieving boy off our hands! Tell the magistrate he tried to steal a purse from Lukar the Merchant. I'll come by later and swear out a complaint."

"Aye, sir!" replied the constable, taking control of John's collar.

The merchant walked away in a huff of rich furs, without a backward look as the constable hauled John off to the magistrate.

It had been a mistake to mention the word 'mage' when he'd been caught, John realized. No one believed him, exactly, but no one was willing to take any chances, either. So they stuck him in a cell underneath the court and told him there he would stay until a mage could be located to evaluate his claim and determine what could and should be done with him.

While being locked up chafed at him, it was John's first hot meal in longer than he cared to think about. So for the first few days he ate and slept and thought and read his *History*, which one of his jailers had been kind enough to let him have from his rucksack. Not being able to read, the man didn't realize he was giving a suspected mage a book on magic.

While in jail, John got the latest gossip and learned

what had happened to cause a full-fledged dragon war since he had last seen Galanoth. Akriloth's attacks on the villages had not been the random acts of a deranged monster after all, but a deliberate attempt to trick the humans into helping him locate a powerful fire orb, which he had then stolen and used to amass an army. By the time Galanoth had arrived at Akriloth's lair, there were hundreds of fire monsters to battle through, and Galanoth and his brave dragon slayers had been hard pressed to contain them, much less to destroy their leader.

That was one comfort; however many days it took him to get out of the magistrate's clutches, it sounded as if there would still be a chance to avenge himself on some dragons when he was set free.

It never occurred to John that it would take more than a few days to resolve his situation. But it was weeks before anything happened. It was going on a full month when a mage was finally located and brought down to John's basement cell. By then the lack of real light had sapped John's will as surely as a lack of any other nutrient. He noticed the effect with disinterest, unable to muster up enough energy to care.

Apparently, with his ability to use light had come an increased sensitivity to its effects. Deprived of the sun long enough, he barely felt like breathing, much less like trying to plan an escape. The ship he had hoped to catch a ride on to Dunderweed had long since set sail, and the ship after that as well. John felt like a caged animal, and had become sullen and silent in his captivity. Once the initial shock of being in jail had subsided, there hadn't been much to do except brood about his losses and berate himself for the choices he had made.

When the mage was let into his cell, John barely spared him a glance, so intent was he on mentally beating himself up for his stupidity in getting caught.

The mage sat watching him for several minutes before he stirred and spoke to John. "I have been on the trail of a young light mage for a while now. You wouldn't happen to know where I could find one, could you?"

John slowly angled his head to look at the mage. The other man wore a dark blue robe embroidered with runes, hood pulled up around his face. A shock of white hair spilled out from the hood, shadowing his features, but John caught the gleam of intelligent eyes.

John shook his head. "No idea."

"They say he can fly, and he powered a boat across the Wolf River with his magic. Not bad for one so young. If, of course, the stories are true."

The words of the merchant rang in his head. *And why would a mage be going around begging and stealing rich men's purses?* He was no mage. He was a joke. The thought was bitter. John shook his head again. "It's not me. I'm just a common thief. You've wasted your time."

The mage looked at John for another long minute, then reached into a pocket and flipped something at John's head. When the younger man reflexively caught it to keep from being bashed in the head, the mage allowed a small smile to cross his face, but said nothing.

John turned the object in his fingers. It was a stone the size of a hen's egg, and started to glow in his hand as he looked at it. Jerking as if he had been burned,

John quenched the power that had wanted to race from him into the stone, and the light went out. Hastily, he put it down on the table and looked at the mage.

"What is that?"

"It's a Duma sun stone. If you were truly a light mage, it would have lit up as soon as you touched it. But I could see it dead in your hand. If ever you did have magic, the heart for it has gone from you as surely as if it had never existed."

There was a moment of silence.

"I'm sorry," the mage said. "There is nothing I can do. You may keep the stone for a novelty, if you like. They have no real value."

Rising, he signaled the guard to let him out of the cell.

Once the mage had been and gone, pronouncing John harmless, John's sentencing had been swift. With no parents to claim him, and the complaint of the merchant to provide proof of his lawless nature, John was ordered to the Krovesport Home for Wayward and Abandoned Children until such time as a relative showed up to claim him, or he reached the age of majority.

The magistrate had stared down at John from underneath a crooked white wig as he consigned John to the home. "You have shown that you cannot walk among the upright citizens of Krovesport and therefore must be supervised and rehabilitated before you are too far gone to be reclaimed, John Black. For the good of your soul and for the good of those around you, you will be remanded to the care and custody of these good people until your sixteenth birthday at which time, if you have truly reformed, you will be released."

Numbly, John let himself be led off. Locked up until he was sixteen? Was that a joke? He couldn't be locked up until he turned sixteen! He had to find Galanoth! He had dragons to kill! Dragons!

John's eyes narrowed as he was led away by two burly guards. It was a cursed dragon that was responsible for all of this. He vowed then and there to kill the first dragon he came across, whether it cost him his own life or not.

“What kind of scrawny vagrant have we caught this time?” said the merchant.

Chapter Three

There were two sets of dormitories in the Krovesport Home for Wayward and Abandoned Children, John learned. Kids who had been abandoned or orphaned, but who were considered basically not a problem, were placed on one of the upper floors on the south side, which faced the street. The first floor of the 'home' on both sides was where the kitchen, communal dining room and classrooms were; the boys had the next two floors, and the girls were on the very top.

Everyone was expected to take their turn at the never-ending list of chores at the home; there was gardening work, cleaning, cooking and laundry. There was also 'school,' sort of, but it didn't focus much on reading, writing and arithmetic. The residents at the home weren't considered likely to become scholars as they grew older. Instead, a variety of craftsman took a turn at teaching different skills that the kids were eventually supposed to be able to earn a living with.

Classes were held in the morning, with chores in the

..oon. There wasn't much supervision inside the ..., locked home and walled garden during the day. As ..ong as everyone was in bed where they were supposed to be by lights out, the staff didn't pay much attention. It could make things a little scary when one of the bigger kids was looking for trouble.

Kids who were convicted of some kind of crime were considered 'wayward' or 'incorrigible' and were placed on the north side, which faced a huge, walled garden. John was considered both orphaned and incorrigible, but found out that incorrigible trumped orphaned, so he was assigned to the north side of the building.

He was put in a second floor-room with two other beds and given back his rucksack, minus his knife and his tinder kit.

After feigning a limp, he was even able to convince them he needed his staff back. After weeks without touching it, the goldenrod felt cool and powerful in his hand, and he thought of the stone the mage had given him. A Duma sun stone? Was that the same as a light stone as described in his book? First, he'd have to finish stripping the staff of its heavy, honey-colored bark, then figure out how to bind the stone to it. Setting the staff next to him, he lay back on his narrow bunk. Maybe later. If his new roommates didn't kill him first.

When he'd arrived, the dorm had been empty. The tired old man who'd admitted him and let him have his staff back said that the other residents were outside, tending the large vegetable garden that supplied the school. John was mildly surprised. He'd seen the big wall, thick and tall, that ran around the home's grounds and made it look like a fortress; it hadn't occurred to him that anything as wholesome as a vegetable garden would be inside.

All too soon, there was the bang of a door flying open at the rear of the building, and then a rush of sound: laughter, shrieks, shouting, and riding over it all a shrill whistle, repeated frequently. John felt a clenching in his gut – the rest of the residents had returned from their gardening chores, and he was about to meet his new roommates. Deciding to postpone the moment he dreaded as long as possible, John rolled over onto his side and closed his eyes. *I'll pretend to be asleep*, he thought to himself, *until I figure out what they're like*. He curled his fingers around the staff that lay next to him, just in case.

He shouldn't have even bothered pretending, he thought with disgust a couple of minutes later. The door flew open with enough force to make the walls shake, and a loud voice boomed, "Hey, Lafe! New roommate! Hey, who are you?"

John's bed buckled, and John realized the owner of the voice had sat down on the side of it. Reluctantly, he rolled over and opened his eyes.

To find himself staring directly into the eyes of a troll, only inches away from his own.

John bolted upright, and let out a small shriek.

The troll made a triumphant sound and his face retreated a few inches.

"He's scared," said the troll. "Did you hear him? He screamed like a girl."

"No I didn't," said John, although he still managed to scoot a few inches further away as he spoke.

"Then what was that noise you just made?"

"I … ah … I was sleeping, that's all. I must have been having a nightmare. That's what it was."

"So a bad *dream* made you scream like a girl?" Somehow, the troll made it sound even wimpier than being scared by … a troll.

"Give it up, kid," advised a bored-sounding voice from across the room. "The sooner you admit he scared you silly, the happier he'll be."

John dared to look away from the troll to see a tall, slender teenager in a dark tunic and leggings leaning against a chest on the opposite wall. A gold earring dangled from one ear. Even though he didn't look much older than John, he already had a small tuft of dark hair growing below his lower lip. He was digging dirt out from under his nails with a knife.

"Hey, how'd you get one of those in here? I had to practically convince them my leg had been cut off just to get a walking stick."

So fast he hardly saw the movement, the guy on the chest flipped the knife and sent it flying though the air toward John's head. It barely missed his ear as it pierced the wall, where it hung quivering.

The troll turned to look at the knife-thrower. "And you think I'm scaring him?"

The guy who had thrown the knife straightened up, then walked over to pluck the knife from the wall and looked down at John. "Hey, kid. No questions about my armament and we'll get along fine. I'm Lafe. This walking mountain here is Tinker."

The troll grinned. "Actually, I'm just half-troll. I got these gorgeous baby blues from my human father." He batted his eyes like a girl and, despite himself, John snickered.

"I'm John Black. All human, all trouble, all the time."

"Join the crowd," said Lafe, joining them on the bed and pulling one leg under himself, tailor fashion.

"You guys both orphans, too?"

Tinker shifted slightly, but didn't say anything, suddenly busy looking at the wall.

"He's a little sensitive, kid. His dad's family didn't want him cause he was part troll, and his mother's tribe didn't want him because he was part human. When his dad's ship went down with all hands, there was no place for him to go but here."

"I'm not a kid. I'm just small for my age."

"Didn't mean to offend. Sorry."

"Apology accepted. How about you?"

Lafe shrugged. "No one knows where my mom is. My dad's a mercenary. He left to go join the fight in the dragon war, and I … got into some trouble here at home. They locked me up until he comes back and gets me."

"My parents both died in a dragon attack," John volunteered. He hadn't planned on telling anyone anything. But these guys felt different. Like he could trust them.

Lafe looked interested, Tinker shocked. "Around here?"

"Nah. We lived in one of the first villages to get attacked. I wasn't home when the dragon came. Far as I know, I'm the only survivor. Galanoth the Dragon Slayer found me, gave me a ride to the next village over, but I hated it there and took off. Been traveling ever since."

"You met Galanoth?" said Tinker, visibly impressed.

"Yeah. I just heard about how there was a full-fledged dragon war going now, and came to Krovesport to try and catch a ride on a ship down to Dunderweed so I could fight too. Then I got arrested … And here I am."

"Huh," said Lafe, thoughtfully. He looked at Tinker. "You thinking what I'm thinking?"

"I don't know," replied Tinker. "I don't know what you're thinking."

Lafe made an impatient noise. "The kid's right. What are we doing hanging around this dump when we could be fighting in the war?"

"I'm not a kid," said John.

"Yeah, yeah. Think about it, Tinker. We could bust out of this joint, hitch a ride on the first ship outta here, and go join the battle. Something to do, right? Whaddaya say? Maybe I could even find my old man."

Tinker looked thoughtful. "How do we swing getting a ride on a ship? The quackers will be looking for us the minute they realize we're gone. And we'll need money, or a good plan to sneak onto one of the ships in the harbor."

"Quackers?" asked John.

"Yeah, quackers – you know the name for this place, right?" asked Lafe.

"Sure. The Krovesport Home for Wayward and Abandoned Children, right?"

Lafe grinned. "Exactly. K-H-W-A-C. Quack. Which makes this the Quacker Factory, and the staff the quackers."

"What's that make us?"

Tinker answered. "We're the Corrs. For 'incorrigibles.'"

"The Corrs and the quackers?"

"Exactly. Congratulations, kid. You've just joined the ranks of the incorrigibles."

Lafe spit in his palm and held it out. After a moment's hesitation, John did the same. Tinker followed suit and placed his huge mitt over both of theirs. John cringed only slightly at the huge amount of spit produced by a troll doing a handshake vow.

"To the Corrs!"

"To the Corrs!"

"To the Corrs!"

By the end of the first week, John had a sunburn on his back, blisters on his hands, and two roommates who felt like brothers. They fell asleep every night talking bout how they'd all ended up in the Quacker Factory, and what they were going to do when they got out.

The first problem, Lafe figured, was to get some accurate information. "It's no good getting out of here if we end up sitting around on the dock with no place to go," he pointed out. "We need to find out when the next ship is leaving, and reconnoiter it so we can find a hiding place for this big lunk," he said, gesturing to Tinker with the point of his knife.

"Makes sense," said John, "But how are we gonna manage that? We don't have anything to bribe one of the quackers with, and who else could we get to go find out for us?"

Lafe broke into laughter. "Kid, when I say *we*, I mean us. Not some quacker that we bribe."

"I'm not a kid. And how are *we* gonna do that when we're stuck in here?"

Lafe shrugged. "We're out there working in the garden every day, aren't we?"

"So?"

Tinker joined the conversation. "I think I see where you're goin' with this. We dig a tunnel, then we can come and go how we want, right?"

Lafe nodded. "Sort of. Except, I was thinking more of a door than a tunnel. I don't like gettin' dirty."

"How are we going to make a door in the wall around this place?" asked John.

Lafe grinned. "Simple, kid. I've been reading your book."

"I'm not a kid. You've been reading my magic book?"

"Sorry. Yeah. And I've been learning a lot."

"For instance?"

"Well, for one thing, I know why you keep flying through the air when you throw a light ball at the ground."

"Huh. How come?"

"Because that ball of light is full of light energy, and even though it looks like it left your hand, you're still connected to it. So, when it hits the ground, it pushes with all the light energy in it. But since it can't move

Lore, it moves you."

John nodded. "Makes sense."

"Yep. But that's not all I learned. Look, I think you should finish up your staff thingy there, get your stone hooked up, and give it a try. Between Tinker's muscles and your magic, I think we can open a door in the wall, and can go back and forth whenever we want, with no one the wiser."

John frowned down at the ground. "Every time I try to do magic, all I do is scare chickens and kill fish."

"Not true. I saw you get up in the middle of the night last night. You had a light, and you weren't carrying a lantern. That's handy."

"And I saw you pushing a pencil around the table the other day with a little marble of light that came back to you when you rolled it away," chimed in Tinker. "How did you scare the chickens?"

John shrugged, unaccountably embarrassed. "I was trying to impress a mage."

"No kidding?"

John looked up and grinned. "Swear. Except it backfired somehow. The mage who apprenticed me? I landed on his hen house the first day I met him, and destroyed the whole thing. Plus, I set his roof on fire."

"*Boulders!* That must have been awesome!"

Remembering the look on Qilder's face when he had crawled out from under the porch and surveyed the damage, John had to snicker. It was the first time since the dragon attack that the thought of Qilder hadn't made him feel sad.

"So," said Lafe, plunging ahead, "when are you gonna be ready to customize that staff of yours? Turn it into a real mage's staff?"

That was something John hadn't thought about since he'd arrived. Reflexively, he gripped the handle of his goldenrod staff and again felt the power inside him straining to rush into the staff and fill it with light.

"I don't know how," he said honestly.

Lafe grinned. "It's okay, kid. Like I said, I've been reading the book. And if we're gonna pull this off, you're gonna need your staff."

"I'm not a kid. So, help me figure out what to do."

Between John's instinctive understanding of how his power worked and Lafe's ability to read and, more importantly, understand the text of the *History*, work on John's staff was finally able to proceed. He peeled away the bark, exposing the glowing white wood underneath – wood that seemed to pulse with its own inner light, even before he was ready to begin carving the runes of power and focus on its gleaming surface.

At that point, the staff stood out too much to hide effectively from others, and work had to be stopped while Lafe deciphered what the *History* had to say about hiding magic. To John's surprise, he learned that there was a parallel process to creating light, which was absorbing light. Once he learned how to apply the principle to his staff, he was able to remove the light from it to store inside himself, and the staff looked like any other dingy piece of discarded wood until John poured his power back into it.

Rather like what he had done with the Duma sun stone when the mage had tried to trick him into revealing his abilities, he realized with some surprise. He had just done it so instinctively, he hadn't known exactly what had happened.

Thinking of that reminded John of the sun stone again, so he pulled it from the pouch he had taken to wearing around his neck and concentrated on pouring light into it as he held it in his hands.

"*Daggers!*" exclaimed Lafe, as he whipped his blanket off his bed and tossed it over John's lap.

"What?"

"It's that light! You're going to give the whole thing away, kid!"

Belatedly, John looked around and realized that while he had been sitting on his bed, full night had fallen. He looked down at his hands, where – even covered by Lafe's blanket – the Duma stone shown with the brilliant light of a miniature sun, and winced.

"I'm not a kid, and sorry. I wasn't thinking."

"I guess not! I said your name three times! It was like you were in a trance or something."

"That thing you did with the stone was pretty amazing, though, John," said Tinker. "We keep hanging out with you, we're gonna need to pick up some eye shades!"

"Yeah, it was pretty bright, huh?" said John, pleased.

"Pretty bright is an understatement," said Lafe. "We're gonna have to get some covers for the windows and for under the doors, too, if you're gonna keep working in here at night. We can't take a chance on somebody seeing the light and squealing."

There was a knock on the door, and all three of the roommates froze.

"I think it's too late," whispered Tinker.

John had an absurd impulse to pretend they weren't there, which made no sense. If the quackers thought they had taken off, they'd be in even more trouble than they would be for doing unauthorized magic in the dorm. Although he couldn't imagine exactly what the consequence for that would be. He didn't remember seeing any rules about it on the big rule board in the dining room. Reluctantly deciding to face whoever was at the door, he slid the now dark stone back into its pouch and stood up.

Just as he put his hand on the doorknob, there was another knock, this one faster and quieter than the other. It gave him courage – whoever was out there didn't want to get caught, either.

He pulled the door open, and before he could even blink, a slim figure completely covered in a scarlet cloak had slipped by him into the room.

The figure turned and pushed the door shut, then pushed back the dark red hood.

A girl stood there, with smooth pale skin and a cloud of dark hair. Green eyes glinted in the lamp light.

"Hey," she said. "I saw your light on. Can I come in?"

No one made a sound for a full minute. John glanced around and saw that Tinker and Lafe's mouths were both open, then realized his was, too. Shutting it with a snap, he shook his head to clear it. "Yeah, sure. I mean, come on in. Have a seat?"

He indicated the study desk they shared, which had a larger-than-usual chair due to Tinker's larger-than-usual size.

"Ah, actually, " she said, flicking those brilliant green eyes around the room, "if you had someplace I could just hide for a few minutes, that would be great."

"Hide?" repeated John, not sure if he'd heard right.

Lafe was a little quicker, now that he'd gotten his mouth closed. "Here, behind the cloaks," he hissed, and opened the wardrobe door.

She'd barely gotten herself tucked away when there was a tramp of heavy, booted feet in the hallway. There was one loud knock, and then their door was thrust open without waiting for a reply.

It was the night guard and two burly matrons from the girls' floor.

They pushed through the open door and surveyed the room with suspicion.

"You!" barked out one of the women. "Have you seen a girl down here?" She pointed a gnarled finger at John, who shook his head.

The other woman bent over to look under the beds, the night guard looking on.

The first woman sneered in Tinker's direction. "She's not here, Mal. If she'd come in here we'd have heard her shriekin' a mile away when she caught sight of that one's face."

Tinker blinked, looking startled.

The night guard walked over and pulled open the wardrobe, which was crowded with Tinker's cloak alone, not to mention John and Lafe's. John thought he detected a thin sliver of scarlet in their midst, but that was all. Tinker's cloak was long and hung to the floor of the wardrobe, where John could barely make out four pairs of boots.

Snarling, the first matron swept out of the room, followed by the second matron and the boys' dorm night guard. Lafe walked to the door and opened it silently, then looked up and down the corridor. John could hear a faint staccato rapping of knuckles from down the hall, followed by the gravelly, demanding voice of the matron.

Lafe shut the door and they all relaxed marginally.

Tapping on the wardrobe, John whispered, "they're off bothering someone else. You can come out, now."

As regally as a queen departing her throne, the girl in the scarlet cloak stepped down from the wardrobe. "Hi," she said when she'd reached the floor and was standing coolly in front of them. "I'm Merridi. Pleased to meet you."

Sitting at the desk, Merridi explained that she'd snuck out to the garden for some fresh air and had spied the light glowing brightly from their window. Before she could decide what to make of it, the alarm had sounded and she knew she'd been found out, so she'd made a beeline for the only place she thought she might find help – whoever had made that awesome beacon of light from the second floor boy's dorm.

"I was just telling him we needed to get some coverings for the window," said Lafe.

"Who?" asked the girl.

"John," Lafe replied, nodding at the young man in question. "He's a full-fledged light mage. He just needs to practice. We're going to break out of here and go join the dragon wars to the south."

Merridi flinched.

"Don't worry, we're not *that* incorrigible. We're going to fight on the side of the dragon slayers, not the dragons," said John.

"Of course."

"But right now, we better find a way to sneak you back upstairs while they're still searching down here. Maybe you can make it look like some stupid mistake or something," said John.

"The last girl they caught off the grounds got sent back to the magistrate," Merridi said. "I heard she's in one of those cells under the court."

She shuddered and John sympathized. He wouldn't want to go back there, either.

"Although, if it looks like I never got downstairs at all …" Merridi drifted off thoughtfully.

Lafe nodded. "It could work."

"But how could I get back up there without them seeing?"

"Which room is yours?" asked Lafe.

She thought for a moment. "On this side, five windows to the left, as you're looking out."

John grinned. "You're not afraid of a little magic, are you?"

Just then Tinker, who'd been looking preoccupied

during the entire conversation, spoke up. “You really think I could scare someone just by showing them my face? No growling or showing my teeth or anything?”

Merridi looked at him intently for a moment, then smiled and laid a palm on his cheek. “Absolutely. Tinker, you’re definitely the scariest guy I’ve ever met.”

Tinker beamed. Behind his back, Lafe rolled his eyes, and John grinned.

Then he got serious. If he was going to use magic to get Merridi back upstairs in the next few minutes, he had some serious work to do.

After some heated debate on the best way to accomplish their goal, they decided to use their sheets, blankets, and cloaks to make a long, thick rope, and tied it to one of Tinker’s boots.

Watching to make sure no one was out in the back yard to see them, Tinker tossed the weighted end up onto the shallow roof until it hooked around one of the roof’s many heavy stone gargoyles and stayed firm. Carefully, Tinker edged out the window, the other end of the rope tied around his waist. When they were sure it would hold, Merridi climbed out after him, then hopped up onto his broad shoulders. When they were settled, John sent a tiny ball of light arcing out his fingertips and bouncing off Tinker’s tough hide.

The rope started to swing, but the light threw out sparks. Closing his eyes, John pictured the ball of light, hidden inside a larger ball of – *unlight*, he decided. He opened his eyes and saw a small dark globe resting on the tips of his fingers. John gently lobbed the second ball, which did its job without showing any light, and the rope swung harder. Then another. One more, and he could see Merridi reaching for the lip of rock that projected out above her window. She couldn't quite make it the first time, but now Tinker had some momentum going and the rope's arc was taking on a life of its own. On the next swing, Merridi caught the rock lip in agile fingers and swung up to stand on the ledge outside her window. A tug at the frame, and Lafe and John watched her disappear inside just moments before a light appeared in her room. Quickly, they caught Tinker as he swung by and reeled him in.

It was up to Lafe, the most agile of the three, to sneak up to the attic and onto the roof, untangle Tinker's shoe weight from the gargoyle and bring back their sheets and blankets. As Lafe himself had pointed out, though, the staff had been looking for an escaped girl heading *down*, not an already accounted-for boy heading *up*.

The next morning, John looked but didn't see Merridi in the communal dining room, or the next. It was Tinker, of all people, who finally found out what had happened. He got the info from one of the girls that tended the garden near his own spot. Merridi had them half-convinced that they had looked in the wrong room initially when they did their nightly head-count on the girl's floor. After all, she'd been safely tucked into bed when they'd gone back. And unlike the boy's floor, where everyone had to share, the girl's incorrigible wing was empty enough for everyone to have their own rooms; there'd been no one there to tell on her.

But just in case, the matron had given her a painful whipping with a cherrup tree switch, and grounded her to her room with only watered milk and bread to eat for a week.

Exactly seven days after Merridi had hidden in their wardrobe, John was sitting in the dining room with Tinker and Lafe when Merridi strolled by, gleaming green eyes as blank as if she'd never seen them before in her life. He felt a surge of disappointment. But when he looked down, there was a carefully folded piece of paper in his lap that hadn't been there a moment ago. Opening it up, he read a single line of hastily scrawled words. His lips moved silently as he read them. *Thank you. See you all tonight.*

John looked up and saw Merridi's eyes on him from across the room. She winked, and then turned back to say something to the girl standing next to her.

John grinned as he passed the note to Lafe. Life had just gotten a lot more interesting.

Chapter Four

That night as John, Tinker, and Lafe hung out in their rooms speculating about when Merridi would show up, there was a tapping at the window. John opened it and a small, weighted string flew in. He stuck his head out and looked up to see Merridi leaning out her window, waving and making pulling motions. Obligingly, he tugged on the string until there was a small pile on the floor followed by the tail-end of a rope ladder.

Once the end of the rope ladder was in the room and tied off on Tinker's bed frame, Merridi herself followed shortly, climbing nimbly down the ladder.

When John looked through the window, he could see the other end of the ladder was anchored in her room.

Merridi followed his glance. "I found some rope up in one of the storage rooms," she explained. "I think there's enough to make another one that can go from this room to the ground."

Lafe shrugged. “Or, Tinker can jump down and catch us. He’s good at jumping, huh, Tinker?”

Tinker nodded. “Not a problem. Trolls are excellent jumpers.”

“Really?” said Merridi. “I had no idea. Makes sense though, I guess, all that mountain climbing and everything.”

Tinker nodded. “Fortunately, I take after my mother’s side of the family.”

Merridi laughed.

“Are you afraid you’ll get caught again?” asked Tinker of Merridi.

“I found a nyxie plant in the garden. I slipped a leaf into the matrons’ tea to make them sleep. They’re both up there snoring like drunken old rogues!”

She looked at John expectantly. “Do you think you could do your *unlight* trick to hide the ladder?”

He looked at the ladder thoughtfully, then put a hand on the rope and imagined a thin sheen of *unlight* flowing up the ladder and into Merridi’s room.

When he blinked and looked toward the window, the rope ladder was nowhere to be seen. John turned back, to see Lafe, Tinker and Merridi all looking at him with amazement. He glanced down and realized that even the portion of the ladder that was in the room had disappeared. If he looked very closely, he could see a small … ripple … where the ladder should have been. And he could still feel it, stiff and prickly, under his hand. He realized that *unlight* was not dark, so much as it was a bending *away* of the light, somehow.

They all looked at the ladder – rather, the *absence* of a ladder – and then looked at John, who was staring at his own hand, baffled and pleased.

"Wow, I really did that, huh?"

"Yeah, kid, you really did. That's quite a trick you got there. I wonder what else you can make disappear?"

"I'm not a kid – and let's find out!"

After some experimenting, they determined that John could '*unlight*' inanimate objects and have them stay that way for several hours – the *unlight* would slowly fade away over time. For people, John had to be in fairly close proximity, but he could hide himself. And, as long as they stayed close, either Lafe or Merridi. Tinker was a little too big for him to manage. "But, hey," pointed out Lafe, "a week ago, we didn't even know you could do this. Who knows what you'll be doing in a month?"

Merridi leaned forward from her seat at the desk. "Speaking of what we'll be doing in a month, are you guys still planning on busting out of here?"

John gave her as serious a look as he could manage while juggling four small balls of light. "Actually, the place has been kind of growing on us. I was thinking about sticking. Maybe get a job here. You, Lafe?"

"Been thinkin' about it. Food's pretty good."

Tinker looked at Merridi with a sorrowful face. "I can't go without Lafe and John. They'd get creamed in here without me."

Merridi looked down at her feet, then back at the three boys. "Then I guess I it doesn't matter that I blabbed to the matron that you were going, huh?"

"What? What? You told them?" all four balls of light dropped to the floor, then slowly melted, as John flung out his hands in shock.

She looked at all three of them, one by one, right in the eye. And then, very slowly, she winked.

"John, you are so gullible!"

"That was a joke? *Suns!* I totally thought you were serious."

Tinker grinned. "Merridi would never give us away."

Lafe angled a look at Tinker. "What makes you so sure of that, big guy?"

"She's a Corr, Lafe, just like us. Nobody ever came around asking why we hid her, did they? And she got whipped with a switch."

There was a moment of silence at that, as everyone looked everywhere except at each other. It made John's gut knot just to think about somebody hurting Merridi. He could tell just by looking at them that the other guys felt the same way.

To change the subject, he nudged Tinker. "Hey, did you really mean that when you said that if we stayed, you'd stay?"

"Yeah. Why? Did you think I'd go off and leave you guys?"

John shrugged. "I never thought about it, I guess. I was just surprised when you said it, is all."

"Why are you still here, kid?"

"I'm not a kid, and … I don't know." It hadn't really occurred to John that he could just leave although, now that he thought about it, he could probably just pop himself over the wall any time he wanted to. But … "You know, the thing is, I until I met you guys, I didn't know what to do anymore. I mean, if I left, I'd just get picked back up again before I could get out of town. I guess I kinda … gave up. You know?"

Merridi nodded. "Me, too. I guess if I put my mind to it hard enough, I could have figured out some way out of here, but I didn't have anywhere to go if I did."

One by one, they all looked at Lafe, who rolled his eyes. "Okay, I couldn't do it without you guys, either. Now, can we start talking about an escape plan, or are we gonna hang around saying how much we need each other all night?"

During the course of several clandestine meetings, they decided that Lafe's plan – to sneak out and find out what they could about ships leaving the harbor, and the best method of stowing away – gave them the greatest chance of success. None of them wanted to play hide-and-seek around Krovesport with the constables while waiting until a ship sailed. The consequences if they were caught were too great.

Every night, as Merridi and Lafe discussed exactly what they were going to do, Tinker listened patiently and watched John create light shows in their room. One evening, they all stopped talking to watch as John created a thick coating of light on one hand and then let it slowly ooze down his fingers to drip on the floor, where it formed a viscous puddle. Merridi shook her head. "If anyone had ever told me that light could look disgusting, I wouldn't have believed them. But that looks like … glow-in-the-dark snot. It's really gross."

John bowed from the waist. "I do my best."

"You know," Lafe said, "your best isn't half bad anymore, John. I think we ought to work on getting your staff finished before we bust out of here."

John frowned. "I need the spells that will attach the stone to the top of the staff, and the runes to carve into the wood to give it power."

Lafe nodded. "I've been thinking about that." He pulled out John's *Brief History of Magic* from a back pocket and opened it to a page he'd marked with a sliver of wood.

They all gathered to read over his shoulder.

Many mages rely on tried-and-true spells to accomplish their goals, but a sufficiently powerful – and sufficiently motivated –- wizard can often achieve the effect they seek by creating their own spells, as long as the purpose is clear and the mage is able to bring the necessary energy to focus when needed.

"In Lorian, now?" said John.

Lafe shrugged. "The way I read it, spells are a way to help concentrate on what you want to achieve, and give you something to focus your power with. But you can write your own. Or we could help you. You don't have to use something somebody else wrote."

"I could write my own? What about the runes?"

Merridi cleared her throat. "I, uh, actually know some of the ancient runes. The T'hark, they're called. I mean, I'm not a professor or anything, but it was part of the required education of – of my family," she finished awkwardly.

They waited for her to go on, but she began looking intently at the book again, and it was obvious that she wasn't going to say anything more. It was the first time Merridi had mentioned her family, and John wondered what had happened that had separated her from them. He was debating whether or not to ask, when Merridi looked up. "If you tell me what you want them to say, I could draw them out for you, and then you could carve them into your staff."

John hesitated. What were magical runes supposed to say? What would he want them to say? "I need to think about it," he concluded. "Can I let you know later?"

"Yeah, sure," said Merridi. "I need to get going now, anyway. See you three tomorrow." And with that, she made her way to the window and scrambled back up the ladder. When she'd passed safely through her own window, Tinker untied the end from where it was hooked around his bedpost and she pulled it up, leaving only the ladder's slender leader thread, which the window could easily be closed on.

The morning after Merridi offered to help John with the runes for his staff, the scheduled class was woodworking. It was taught by a genial carpenter who came in once a week for a small fee and helped the class learn how to build cabinets. Finished cabinets were relegated to the basement or attic, where they were used to store just about anything that could fit in a drawer or on a shelf. Once the class was well underway, John approached him and asked if he could be excused to go to the home's library instead.

Unaware of the staff's take on the uselessness of teaching reading and writing to a bunch of orphans and incorrigibles, upright, well-intentioned members of the community persisted in donating books to the Quacker Factory. While it wasn't very well organized, it gave do-gooders a nice feeling to know there was a room full of books in the home called a library, and that seemed to keep everyone satisfied.

The carpenter regarded him with some astonishment, but waved him on. "Ain't nothing in there but books, lad, but you're welcome to 'em."

Gratefully, John made his escape into the cool, dim library, where the quantity of dust seemed to blanket the room in its own special brand of peace and quiet. For a moment, John just stopped and drank in the silence. He couldn't remember the last time he hadn't had at least one other person within a few feet of him, and he'd almost forgotten what it felt like.

Reminding himself he had a job to do, John moved to the shelves, trying to find a section on song, rites, rituals – anything he could use as an inspiration for the spells he needed to create. As he looked, he realized that somewhere along the line, he had stopped having to pronounce words under his breath to make sense of them. Feeling pleased with himself, he found a section that looked promising. Pulling several books off the shelf, he found a dusty desk and chair and began to read.

John was so engrossed in his reading that he didn't notice someone else had entered the library on sneaking feet until something slapped him in the back of the head – hard.

"Ow! What in the name of Lorithia was that?" he said, jumping out of his seat and clapping a hand to the back of his head.

"Hey, runt, whassa matter? Don't you know a love tap when you feel one?" It was Drant, a big, mean kid who enjoyed bulling the smaller, weaker residents. "What happened to your boys? They dump you for some other wimp that needed protection?"

John scrambled away as Drant advanced, hoping he wouldn't need to use his magic to get out of this. Even if it meant taking a beating, it would be better than getting found out as a mage. If that happened, he'd end up right back in the cell under the court, and his chances to make it to Smoke Mountain and join in the battle against the dragons would be zero.

When he felt a shelf against his back, John froze, and glanced left and right, wondering if he could feint his way past the bully and escape.

A big fist shot out and grabbed his tunic, and John felt his heart sink. Too late, and Drant, for all his size, was too fast. John closed his eyes and waited. For the pain. A lot of it.

"Hey, put that kid down!"

John opened one eye cautiously. Drant's fist hovered just in front of his face, but it had stopped moving. Craning around Drant's bulk, John saw Merridi standing in the doorway, looking like she wanted to kick some serious butt.

"Merridi, it's okay. It's between me and Drant," said John weakly, willing her to leave before she got hurt, too.

"That's right, girlie. Go fix your hair or something, before I decide to put you over my lap and give you a spanking."

Even suspended from Drant's choke-hold, John had to roll his eyes. What an idiot!

Merridi didn't seem to think too much of him, either. She snorted.

"Why don't you drop the kid and try, muscle head?"

"I'm not a kid," said John, as Drant forgot about him and let go. He hit the floor with a heavy thud and rolled, trying to get between Drant and Merridi.

Drant made a move to the left and then plowed forward from the right. Merridi danced away and snapped a quick fist at his head. There was a smacking sound as it connected.

Drant grunted.

He turned and plowed forward again, head down, reminding John of the charge of a bull. Again, Merridi danced away, but this time as she passed Drant, she snapped up her foot and caught him in the chin. He staggered and went down on one knee. Taking advantage of the target Drant presented, John sprang and leaped on his back, knocking him flat and slamming his face into the floor. Hard.

When Drant didn't stir, John grabbed the bully's hair in one hand and pulled, then leaned so he could see Drant's face.

Drant looked for all the world like he had just decided to take a nap on the library floor.

There was a small noise, and John looked up to see Merridi laughing. She held out a hand to help him off

Drant's back.

"Good job, John. I guess we showed him that size isn't everything, huh?"

"Thanks, Merridi. I was figuring I was in for a rough time. He would have blabbed in a heartbeat if I tried to use my magic."

"Yeah," she said, giving Drant a small shove with her foot. He responded with a grating noise that John realized was a snore.

"I figured that was it, when I saw you weren't clobbering him with a light ball or something. You ready to get out of here?"

"Yeah. Let me put these books back. How'd you know to come find me?"

"I saw him sneaking around the hallway and then he came in here. He's not a good guy. I thought I'd check and see what he was up to."

Companionably, they walked out of the library, leaving Drant stretched out on the floor. Behind them, they heard another snore.

John was still working on exactly how to empower his staff when the Corrs decided to make their first expedition out of the Quacker Factory.

Moments after the last shards of moonlight were blanketed by the horizon, the window slid open and Merridi slipped through.

Lafe nodded. 'Okay, then, gang's all here. Let's get

busy."

One by one, they slithered out the window and down the rope ladder 'til they were all standing on firm ground. Carefully, they skirted close to the wall until they reached the tool shed. In the dim starlight, Merridi's scarlet cloak was black as night.

When they arrived at the tool shed, Tinker gave the lock a tug. "Want me to break it?"

"Nah," said Lafe. "Remember, we're just going out to reconnoiter tonight. I don't want to end up having to wait a couple of weeks to get a ride on a ship and spending the whole time in hiding. We're gonna go out, find out which ships are getting ready to go, and figure out how we can stow aboard. Then we're gonna sneak right back in here and act as good as gold until the time is right. Everybody agreed?'

They all nodded.

"Great," said Lafe. "Kid, can you give me a light?"

Obligingly, John pointed at the lock, and sent a thin stream of light into the keyhole. Lafe produced a thin sliver of metal and jiggled it gently in the lock, bending so his ear was next to it as he worked.

There was a barely audible click and Lafe straightened, a pleased smile on his face. In his hand was the open lock.

From inside the shed, they quickly withdrew a pick and wheelbarrow, and then selected a place on the wall to get to work.

Following Lafe's instruction, John shut his eyes and concentrated a razor thin beam of light on the mortar holding one of the ground-level bricks in place. After a moment, the mortar began to melt and run.

"Hey!" said Lafe. "That's not exactly what I expected. Tinker, get rid of that pick and get a trowel instead, okay, buddy?"

"How come he's *buddy* and I'm *kid*?" said John while they were waiting.

Lafe rolled his eyes. "Because if he gets mad at me, he can kick my butt, kid. Why do you think?"

"Oh. Yeah."

Tinker returned, and at Lafe's instructions, dug a trench alongside the stone blocks where they were working, and used the trowel to scrape the melted mortar there. After three rows, three blocks long, had been freed, Lafe instructed Tinker to wriggle the blocks out of their spot on the wall. John then directed his beam of light to fuse the remaining blocks together, forming a solid arch, and they had a neat doorway through the wall. The same technique worked to turn the pile of blocks into a single large stone as Tinker stacked them back up. Nimbly replacing the "door" once they were on the other side, they were ready to go.

It was fun, John realized. Fun to be out on the streets, a thin film of *unlight* twisting around them, obscuring them just enough to make the rogues and miscreants who preyed on the innocent and weak hesitate. The air smelled better, somehow, because it was *free* air. He felt almost like he was floating, and then Lafe hissed and gave his cloak a jerk, and he realized he was. Forcing himself to concentrate, he brought himself back down to the ground and hurried along with his friends to the wharves of Krovesport. Even though it was late, the docks were lively; a ship had just arrived from Deren and the wharf rats were busy unloading it. There were lanterns everywhere, and John was able to use their light – and the shadows that they cast – to sneak himself and the others dangerously close to the workers to listen to the gossip about what was going on in the busy port.

Luck was on their side, John thought, when they overheard two men talking about a ship departing for Dunderweed in less than a week. A shiver of excitement crept up his spine. A week! One week, and he would be out of the Quacker Factory and heading to Smoke Mountain and the dragon war.

"John!" hissed Lafe again, tugging on John's cloak.

Too late. In his excitement, a small pillow of light had actually formed under his feet, lifting him into the air. While the *unlight* still obscured them from being seen directly, one of the men unloading boxes had stopped and was frowning their way. They froze, but the man lifted a hand and pointed. "Hey, Razer! I think there's someone over there, spyin' on us!"

There was a shout, and then another. Several men approached, clubs and knives in their hands. "Back, back," Lafe said, but Tinker stumbled into a large wooden pallet, and the noise alerted the men to their position.

There was rush, and John suddenly found a large, vicious-looking club coming down directly at his head.

"Get out of the way!" yelled Merridi, giving him a

shove. The club missed John and struck Merridi a bone-shattering crack on the shoulder.

There was a moment of absolute silence, followed by a horrible rending sound.

The men who had rushed them stopped and watched, mouths hanging open, as John forgot about maintaining the *unlight*. Merridi fell to the pavement, clutching her injured shoulder, and John clearly heard one man's voice: "*Krill!* I didn't know it was a girl!"

Then everything else faded into the background as Merridi started to change … and change.

Her skin became mottled and red, then turned to iridescent crimson scales. Her hands clenched and her fingers grew long and skinny, then turned into wicked-looking claws. Her neck elongated, her body thickened and twisted, and she grew … a tail?

In the space of a single breath, the girl John had known was gone, and in her place was a dragon. With Merridi's great green eyes.

She looked at him with those eyes now, full of pain and shame. The dockworkers fled en masse, screaming about dragons disguised as humans.

Before John could react, Tinker reached down and stroked a hand over Merridi's broken shoulder. "You were hurt so bad. What can I do?"

She shuddered, then lifted her head. "It's already healing. I can feel it. Just hide me for a few minutes, please? Once the pain isn't so … distracting … I can change back."

Lafe looked around. "We have to get out of here pretty quick. They'll be back with reinforcements soon. John, hide us."

When John just stood there, staring in disbelief, Lafe grabbed his tunic and gave him a shake. "John! Come on, kid! We've got about ten seconds before those sons-of-zards show back up. And no amount of explaining is going to fix the fact that we were sneaking around the docks with a dragon disguised as a human, during the middle of a major war with the dragons!"

Still in shock, John waved a hand, willing the *un-light* back in place. Tinker wrapped both arms around Merridi and helped her to her feet … or paws, or whatever they were.

"Where are we going?" whispered Tinker, after they had safely escaped the docks and the angry sounding mob that seemed to be growing there.

Merridi was already starting to walk on her own, a slinky, snakelike ripple that made John cringe to see. *One of my best friends is a dragon*, he thought numbly. *She saved me from getting my butt whipped by Drant, then she jumped in front of an angry guy with a club for me.*

"How much longer before you can change back?" whispered Lafe. "We need to get off the streets."

"I'm just about ready, I think," said Merridi, and sure enough, her form started to waver and change. In a few minutes, the girl John knew was walking along beside him, avoiding looking him in the eye.

"I think we need to head back to the school for now. Who's gonna look for a dragon at the Quacker Factory, right?" said Lafe.

Tinker nodded. "Makes sense to me. We can get it all sorted out later. John?"

John nodded. "Whatever you guys think. I don't

know what to do."

Merridi laid a hand on John's arm, and he jerked it away.

"Don't touch me!" he shot out. "It was your kind that killed my parents and destroyed my village. I hate you!"

Walking faster, he took the lead, not caring if they kept up or not.

“In the space of a single breath, the girl John had known was gone.”

Chapter Five

For several days, John avoided Merridi, and Tinker and Lafe left him alone about it, for the most part. Merridi had stayed out of his way, which made him feel even more miserable and angry. He felt horribly tricked by someone he had trusted, not to mention the fact that he had sworn to kill the next dragon he met, or die trying. But he couldn't forget how she jumped in the way of the man with the club and taken the hit that was meant for him, either.

"Maybe," suggested Tinker, after watching John spend most of one evening sitting on his bed with his head resting on his knees, "you should ask her why she did it."

John turned his head restlessly. "Why she made fools of us, or why she saved me? It doesn't matter either way. She's still a dragon. Her kind killed my parents!"

Tinker was silent for a moment, thinking. "If a wild troll came down and smashed your family, would you blame me?"

John shrugged. "I don't know. Maybe. Probably. Are you trying to say I'm not being fair? I don't really care about that, Tinker. She's a dragon, she lied about it, she tricked us all, and that just goes to show that she *is* like every other stinking, lying dragon out there." He stood up, voice rising. "They're *wicking* killers, and they don't care about humans at all, and they're not like us! And it's not about being fair or anything like that. Every time I think about being in the same room with one of those monsters, I get sick to my stomach I want to kill it so bad!"

There was a tap at the window, and they looked to see Merridi peering in. Lafe walked over and slid up the frame and she perched on the ledge. "This a good time?"

"Great!" yelled John. "Just great! Stay away from me!"

Merridi's face froze. "No problem," she said, ice in her voice. "I don't want to inflict myself on anyone." She started to leave, and Lafe grabbed her arm. He nodded at Tinker, who moved between John and the door.

"What the *suns* are you doing?" demanded John, trying to shove past Tinker and not succeeding.

"It's time we got this over with," Lafe said. "You've been brooding for three days."

Tinker pointed a finger at Merridi. "And you've been avoiding us."

She shrugged. "I don't go where I'm not wanted."

"You came down here tonight," John shot back. "I didn't invite you here."

"But Tinker did," she said. "Obviously, it was a

mistake."

"It was a mistake, because you're a lying, murdering dragon!"

"Who saved your life!"

John couldn't figure out how to respond to that one, and he couldn't reach the door because Tinker was blocking it, so he flung himself back onto his bed.

After a brief silence, Merridi and John both said the same words to Lafe at the same time. "What do you want from me?"

Lafe looked like he was struggling to hide a smile, which earned him twin glares.

"We need to talk this out. We're family, right?"

John snorted, and Merridi just looked at the ceiling.

"Thinking beings are not ever all alike just because of where or what they were born as," argued Lafe. "That's the whole point of being a thinking being – thinking about things. I think we should give Merridi a chance to at least explain what's going on."

John said nothing.

"Look, John, we need each other to get out of here. You know that. Just listen to what she has to say. If you decide you still can't stomach working with her after that, fine. We'll get out of here, get on the boat, and once we're far enough away that there's no risk of being sent back to Krovesport, we can each go our separate ways. For right now, though, let's try to find a way to work together and get the *daggers* out of here, okay?"

Tinker nodded. "I heard that there's been a squad organized in town to look for the dragon disguised as a human. They didn't get a good look at any of us, but they're bringing in a tracking sneak."

They all absorbed that information silently. John thought he saw a shudder race over Merridi, and he didn't blame her. Tracking sneaks were relentless. A slithering reptile nearly as smart as a man, a deadly attack, and a sense of smell even better than a Hell-hound's. There'd probably been enough people crossing their path over the last three days to throw off an ordinary dog. And Merridi had changed from dragon to human and even been carried by Tinker for a while. But John didn't think those things would confuse a sneak for long, if what he'd heard about them were true.

He looked at Tinker. "How much time do you think we have?"

"A day, maybe two, from what I heard."

John turned to Merridi and gave her a hard stare. "Okay, time to convince me not to give you up. And it better be good."

"I come from a small, isolated tribe of dragons far north of here," Merridi started. "Shape changing isn't uncommon in my clan, and my people use this ability to trick innocent travelers and rob them – or worse.'

John snorted. "See, I told you. None of them are any good."

Lafe motioned him to be silent.

"Usually, a dragon becomes a shape changer as they get close to adulthood. It starts as something that can only be done with a lot of concentration, and for very short periods of time. There are only a few of us who can maintain a change for extended periods – long enough to entice a traveler into the village, for example. But I've been able to change and stay changed for longer than anyone else in our history. And since I was a girl, I was good for luring people in – who would think a cute little girl would be a monster, right?"

John hissed under his breath, but didn't say anything.

"The thing was, the more I stayed in human form, the more I learned about humans, and the more I liked them. I didn't want to be part of anything that would hurt them. One day, a family was lured into our village and, even though I wasn't involved, I felt horrible at the thought of what was going to happen to them. I couldn't save them all, but I was able to sneak the little girl away and leave her with some well-armed Taladosians who were passing through the region."

She paused for a moment, looking at the wall, as if seeing the scene there.

"I'll never forget the look in the mother's eyes as I took her baby to safety. She was doomed, and she knew it. But she was so grateful that her baby was going to be spared…"

Merridi's eyes filled with tears, but she blinked them away and went on.

"When the others found out what I had done, they locked me up in one of the cages they kept for prisoners. They were afraid I would give away their secret, and tell the humans about the shape-changing dragons hidden in the mountains."

John stirred uneasily. He knew what it was like to be in a cage.

"I was in that cage for three months, before I finally managed to overpower one of my jailers and get away. They had been seeing me as human for so long, they started treating me like one – forgetting that I could change back into a full-size dragon when I was out of the cage and had enough room. We had a fight, and I won, but it was close."

"How did you end up in Krovesport?" Lafe asked, leaning forward.

"The rest of my people were furious that I had escaped, and terrified that I would tell their secret. They sent their best tracker after me, and I've been on the run ever since. I got as far as Krovesport when the dragon war broke out. I didn't have any money, didn't think I could make it past the dragon slayers – plus, they just scare me – and I didn't know how to find any other dragons who might help me. We didn't even tell other dragons about what we could do. Then I got caught stealing food at the market, and put here. It seemed as good a place to hide as any, so here I've been."

John stood up to pace. The other three watched and waited. Finally, he turned to face Merridi.

"Look, I don't know if I can ever get over how I feel about dragons. But this is the second time you've saved me from a beating or even worse. I can't ignore that, either."

He paced some more. "The thing is, I just can't get over how much I hate dragons. I don't know if I ever will. But we need each other to get out of here, and I really want out of here. We have a lot better chance if we're all together."

Lafe nodded. "But do we still really want to go to the battlefields?"

"What do you mean?" asked Merridi.

"Well, unlike John, I don't care if you're a dragon or not. We're friends, and friends help each other out. But you going to Smoke Mountain right now is a suicide gesture. Both sides are likely to try and bump you off!"

"Yeah," said Tinker. "It's probably not a really good idea, Merridi. Is there anywhere else you want to go? One place is as good as another to me."

"Hey!" John objected. "I'm going to Smoke Mountain. I'm going to help get the dragon that killed my parents. Period. End of story."

Tinker gave John a look that made him feel ashamed. "She saved your butt, twice. You owe her."

John flushed. "Maybe."

"You didn't answer, Merridi," continued Tinker. "If you could go anywhere you wanted, where would it be?"

She sat, lost in thought. "Anywhere?"

"Anywhere." Tinker nodded his big head serenely.

"I think the best place in the world must be the School of Thought in Deren."

There was a knock on the door, the night guard telling them it was time for lights out.

"I've got to go," whispered Merridi. She slipped out the window as Tinker blew out the light.

The guard poked his head in and took a look around. "You guys better get that window closed. Supposed to be a chilly one tonight. And there's a monster on the loose. Don't want something slipping in the window while you're sleepin' now, do ya?"

In the spill of light from the hallway, John could barely make out the man's face, but he could sense the glee in his voice. "What kind of monster?'

"Some horrible mutant, I heard. Half human, half dragon. Goes around disguised as a human girl. It was tearing apart a couple of kids and some big guy when it was first spotted. Rippin' 'em limb from limb, blood everywhere. Tore the head right off one, I heard."

"Oh, *daggers*," said Lafe, incredulous.

"No, really," said the guard. "You don't believe me, just you wait and see. They got a trackin' sneak out there now, and they're combing the whole town. They'll be doing this section tomorrow or the next day, if they haven't already found it."

"Sounds like if they do, it's gonna shred them anyway," pointed out Tinker. "Maybe they should just leave it alone?"

"And have a monster lurking in our midst, ripping heads off children and all?" said the guard, sounding truly shocked. "Anyway, they already got it planned out. Got a big cage to drive it into when they find it, already sittin' on a big pile of wood. Soon as it's in the cage, they're gonna light up that bonfire and roast the freakin' mutant alive." He made a smacking noise of appreciation.

"Well, anyways. That's why you should be keepin' your window shut. I gotta get on with my rounds. Good night, boys."

The guard departed, pulling the door shut behind him.

Out of the dark came Tinker's voice. "Well?"
"Okay, okay," said John. "We'll take her to Deren."

With Lafe's help, and some heavy reading in the library, John finally felt like he knew what he needed to do to empower his staff.

Painstakingly, he collected the components he would need: salt, the dried leaf of a *sanare* plant and a gold coin, obligingly stolen by Lafe from the guard's coin purse and crushed to fine dust between Tinker's big hands. Each item was tied in a small pouch and hidden in one of John's pockets, ready for when he would need it.

He needed three small bowls as well, and snuck into the kitchen one morning after breakfast, hoping to nick several of the shallow clay bowls that the lumps of butter were put out in. He was congratulating himself on his success on getting into the kitchen unseen when he turned around and nearly bumped into Drant.

"Well, well, well. If it isn't my old buddy, Johnny. Where's your girlfriend?" asked Drant with a smirk.

"Ain't gonna be able to hide behind her cloak this time, are you, you little son-of-a-zard?"

John gulped. "Hey, Drant. How's it going?"

Drant frowned now, and his eyes got small and hot. "Not so good since you guys rung my bell. I didn't like that, little man, not one bit."

John attempted to slide toward the door, and Drant

put out a big hand against the wall, boxing him in to the left.

John broke into a light sweat and tried to sidle right. "I was really sorry about that, too, Drant. My apologies, okay?" He thought things were going pretty well, apology-wise, and then could feel the smart-aleck in him rearing its sarcastic head. John winced, but couldn't stop himself. "I was wondering one thing, though."

"One last question before you die? What's that, kid?"

"Does it hurt worse when you get your butt kicked by a girl? I mean, really, I was wondering. Because that's never happened to me, and—"

Drant let out a strangled cry of pure rage and grabbed John's tunic in both hands, lifting him up in the air until they were eye-to-eye and nose-to-nose.

Close enough for John to tell that Drant had a really unfortunate problem with his oral hygiene, but he figured that pointing that out would only make a bad situation worse. Instead, he brought up his staff, as hard as he could, between Drant's legs, and had the satisfaction of watching Drant's face, which had been red as a beet and contorted with malice, suddenly go white and surprised.

Drant made a small chuffing sound and his eyes crossed.

His hands slipped off John's tunic, and John dropped gratefully to the floor.

Drant no longer appeared interested in John at all, as both hands were clutching his groin, but just for good measure, John brought the butt-end of his staff down on Drant's left foot – hard.

Drant toppled slowly to the floor. Grabbing a handful of clean bowls off a nearby counter, John raced out the door before Drant could recover and come after him.

It looked like it would probably be awhile.

Lafe dropped a note to Merridi at breakfast, asking her to meet John in the library, then they got to work convincing the staff that John was sick enough to skip class and stay in bed, but not sick enough to go to the infirmary.

Once everyone had left, John took his goldenrod staff, and made his way down to the first floor, covered in *unlight*. To his relief, Merridi was already there. Although he felt his skin itch being that close to a dragon, they sat right next to each other with the *unlight* hiding them, as they poured over John's notes about the runes he wanted to carve into his staff. When Merridi had written them out, John looked at them, and then at her. "When you said this was part of your family's education, was that true?"

She nodded. "Yes. We leave each other messages, carved into trees or rocks with our claws. And we protect ourselves, or charm our traps, with them. It's very basic, but powerful, a kind of magic that works well for us." She smiled. "It's hard to hold a pen in a huge claw."

But that wasn't what John was focused on. "Traps.

You mean traps for people?"

Her chin went up. 'Do you really want to get into this right now?"

John flushed. "Yeah, but I know it's not a good time. You want to watch me do this to make sure I don't screw it up?"

"Sure," she said, and settled back patiently as he produced the small pouches of salt, crushed gold and dry *sanare* leaf, along with a small flask of water and the clay bowls.

Carefully, he placed each of the items he had gathered inside a clay bowl, then added a small amount of water and stirred them with the blade of a knife he had borrowed from Lafe.

When he was done, he dipped a wooden stylus into the first bowl, then used the stylus to paint the symbols he would carve. Salt to channel the powers of the body: strength, endurance and right. Then he dipped his stylus in gold to channel the powers of the spirit: connection, illumination, hope. Finally, using the healing leaf of the *sanare* plant, he drew the runes that would channel the power of the mind: wisdom, justice, patience.

When he had finished, he took the small knife, finely honed, to carve the three rune sets painted in the glowing wood.

Honor - So I will act in all things
Strength - So I will do in all things
Mercy - So I will show in all things

As he traced the final line of the final rune with his knife there was a brilliant flare of light, and the runes burst into a white-gold flame that burned without charring the wood. He reached for his pouch and drew out the sun stone, balancing it on the top of the staff. The white light from the runes flared again, this time flowing up and down the staff in slender tendrils, capturing the sun stone and anchoring it in place. The sun stone reacted with a blinding flare of white light that faded as quickly as it had flashed into being.

There was silence as John looked at the staff in his hand, now ordinary wood, the runes he had carved barely visible through an intricate design of vines and leaves. The stone was anchored to the staff by more vines, and looked as if it had been there since the branch had first been taken from its tree.

"*Shards*," said Merridi. "That was amazing. Thank you for letting me be a part of that, John."

John flushed, partly embarrassed, partly awed. He could feel the power in the staff and stone, and he could feel the power in himself when he held it, a barely there tingle that he knew now could become a torrent if he willed it.

"You mean those things, don't you?" said Merridi.

John looked at Merridi, having no idea what she was talking about.

"You could have chosen anything to carve on your staff. Revenge. Hate. Death," she said. "But you chose Honor, Strength and Mercy."

"Yeah, well, how many girls can I get with a staff that has all that negative stuff on it?"

She smiled. "I think we'll be alright after all."

It wasn't a question, it was statement. "What do you mean by that?"

She looked at him. "I'm not bad or evil, John. I did the best I could, and when I realized I should do better, I did. You'll see. It may take awhile, but you'll see. You're too smart not to, and too honest not to admit it to yourself when you do."

"Maybe." John let out a breath. He hated being angry, hated hating anyone as much as he hated the dragon that had killed his family – as much as he had hated Merridi when he first realized what she really was. But he didn't know how to make it go away, either.

Merridi was about to say something else, when there was a shout in the hallway.

"Hey! They're in here! I can't see 'em, but I can hear 'em talking!"

John whirled to see Drant smirking in the doorway.

"Turn off the *unlight*," Merridi whispered urgently. "There's no way out. If they see your magic, it will just make things worse."

There was a hiss, and a tracking sneak slithered in, tongue darting in the air, body as thick as a man's thigh. It left a thin trail of slime as it passed, and John noticed that the men who followed were careful where they put their feet. He stepped in front of Merridi and shoved the staff between them, where it couldn't be seen from the door. Quickly, he quelled the *unlight*.

Drant, who had been watching the sneak, glanced up and narrowed his eyes. "Where did you guys come from? You got a hiding place in here or something?'

There was a shout from one of the men. "Hey, it's one of the kids from the dock! He wasn't being attacked, he was helping the dragon!"

The air became thick with curses and cries of "Spies!" "Get them!" But the men in the forefront hung back, apparently hesitant in case Merridi changed form again.

There was a disturbance, and Tinker shoved his way through the crowd, Lafe at his side.

"Hey, kid, watch where you're goin'," said one of the men in the room, then got a look at Tinker and shut up.

Lafe and Tinker crossed the room to where Merridi and John were cornered, and turned to stand with them in front of the crowd. There was an ugly mutter.

"Merridi, how fast can you turn?" muttered Lafe out of the side of his mouth.

"Not fast enough for this. And while I'm turning, I'm pretty helpless."

"Okay, then. John, it's up to you."

"What's up to me?"

"To get us out of here! Come on, how about some of the ol' Johnny-boy razzle-dazzle?"

John frowned. "I'm not a boy. Give me a minute to think."

"Got it," said Lafe.

While John scrambled for an idea, Lafe took a step forward and addressed the angry crowd. The tracking sneak was hissing and weaving at the front, as if looking for the best target to strike. Behind it, the crowd had continued to swell as more people pushed in the doorway, shoving the men in front inadvertently closer.

"You've got the wrong guys, you know," began Lafe, stalling for time. "We're just a bunch of kids."

"The tracking sneak led us right here! How do you explain that?"

"I have a mouse in my pocket?"

The Sneak feinted with its broad, blunt head, and

Lafe jumped out of its way. "Okay, no mice jokes. But look at us! Do we look like we could be up to anything bad?"

There was a moment of silence as the crowd took in Merridi in her crimson cloak, Tinker standing huge as a mountain beside her. They looked at Lafe, in his dark leather pants and tunic, a small tuft of hair growing just below his lower lip, a gold earring dangling from one ear. And John, small, skinny, with a shock of blond hair and large hazel eyes.

"Maybe not all of you," conceded one man.

"Yeah, let the little kid go," called another.

"I'm not a kid!" exclaimed John.

"Then you better come up with something quick," hissed Merridi, "because you were the only one they were going to let go!"

Hand grasping his staff, John pulled it out from behind his back and held it aloft. He felt the power flowing back and forth from himself to the Duma stone that crowned it. The stone glowed brightly as a beacon. "*Unlight!*" he cried.

For an instant, the stone flared brighter, and the crowd cringed back. Then the light went out, and the stone was just another rock, the glowing staff just another piece of dirty wood. There was a titter, followed by a guffaw.

"He *is* just a kid!" someone said, laughing.

Then a shadow passed over the room, and the light grew dimmer. The laughter stopped.

The room got darker. The crowd grew still.

Another second, and the room was as dark as the blackest midnight. "I can't see!" someone yelled.

"He's blinded us!"

"Quick," said John. "Let's get out of here while they can't see!"

They kept one eye on the seething dark curtain that seemed to have fallen between them and the crowd, as they backed toward the windows. Tinker picked up a chair and busted out the window glass, then turned and picked up Merridi by the waist and set her safely outside on the grass.

"*Daggers!*" exclaimed Lafe. "Look!"

John turned his head and saw the tracking sneak sliding forward, dripping the *unlight* as it moved away from the crowd, tongue flickering as it made its way slowly toward them.

"It's finding us by smell," Lafe exclaimed. "It doesn't need to see to know where we are. Hurry!"

"No," said John. "You first."

Lafe looked at the sneak, then at the window. "If you insist," he said, and hopped out to join Merridi.

John opened his mouth to tell Tinker to go next, but before he could say anything, Tinker picked him up bodily and tossed him out the window behind Lafe. John rolled to his feet and returned to the window, just in time to see the sneak make a strike at Tinker. It was a big sneak, ripe with undulating muscle, and the strike was hard enough to topple a full-grown man, fast enough to get by the solid defenses even Tinker had.

The half-boy, half-troll didn't bother trying to evade.

The sneak hit Tinker's rock-like chest and collapsed to the floor, head wobbling. One of the sneak's vicious-looking fangs made a faint pinging noise as it fell to the floor. Even the deadly fangs of the sneak were no match for Tinker's tough hide.

John cheered and Tinker gave him a cheery grin and started to wedge himself through the window.

His smile faded when he was halfway through.

"What's the matter, Tinker?" said John.

"I think I'm stuck. You guys go. I'll be right behind you as soon as I work my way out."

"Not a chance!" said John. "Here, hold still."

Pointing the staff, he recreated the intense beam of light he had used to melt the mortar on the garden wall. Passing through staff and stone, its power was increased tenfold.

Directing the beam at the wall, the light made the bricks sizzle and crumple away. In a flash, the window frame Tinker was stuck in was free and he broke loose, crashing through the remains of the wall with the window frame handing loosely around his neck. He crushed the frame with his big hands as if it were made of toothpicks instead of big slabs of wood.

"Hurry," Tinker said, heading for the back wall where the stones were loose. "I think the sneak was starting to come around."

"Oh, I'd stop right there," said a lazy voice.

John looked around and saw a thin, foppish man wearing a crimson cloak like Merridi's. With one hand, he fiddled with a locket around his neck. At the sight of the stranger, Merridi's face went pale. "Barstow. I knew it was just a matter of time. But there's no reason to bother my friends. It's just me that you want."

"True. Just you."

Merridi relaxed marginally.

"And anyone you've told your secret to."

"Is this the hunter?" asked John

Merridi nodded, eyes never leaving the man as he sauntered forward to stand in front of them.

"And you are the mage, and you the muscle." He nodded at John and Tinker.

Then he turned curious eyes on Lafe. "Then you must be the brains of this pathetic outfit."

John shifted, pointing the tip of the staff toward the hunter.

"Oh," said Barstow. "I wouldn't do that if I were you."

"Oh, yeah? Why not?"

"Because I have a charm here, made by a dragon sorcerer. If you harm the charm in any way, Merridi will suffer accordingly. Isn't that right, girl?"

His features twisted for a split second as he grasped the locket around his neck and squeezed. Merridi gasped in pain, and the hunter sneered.

"Unfortunately, I had to get rather close for it to take effect, but now that I'm here, I think you'll drop that staff and the four of us will go someplace nice and quiet."

There was a noise from the front of the building. With despair, John realized that the effect of the *unlight* was decreasing on the part of the mob furthest from him, and some of the crowd had come out of the home and were making their way around the building.

The hunter tapped his thumb on the locket, and Merridi flew back as if struck.

"Okay, okay, don't hurt her!" said John, and held out his staff for the hunter.

The hunter reached out to take it then jerked, an astonished look on his face. A knife had appeared out of nowhere; buried to the hilt between the toes in one booted foot, it anchored him to the ground where he stood.

In the hunter's split second of shock, Lafe had vaulted behind him and now held another knife to the man's throat. "Just because I'm the brains of this outfit doesn't mean I can't take care of myself and my friends, dragon breath," he said. He whipped up the knife as the man cringed, and cut through the leather thong that held Merridi's charm around his neck.

He tossed it to Merridi, who caught it neatly.

"Now," said Lafe, "can we please get out of here?"

Tinker grinned. "About time!"

They flew down the garden and Tinker was just pushing out the 'door' from the wall as the crowd rounded the building and saw them. They raced through the opening.

"Hurry, Tinker! Come through and get the door set back in there! Quick!" said Lafe.

"Sure," said Tinker, moving to do as Lafe said, "but they'll just take it back out."

Lafe gestured to John. "Not when the wizard does his stuff!"

Holding out his staff, John once again poured his power through it and into the sun stone, directing the intense beam around the edge of the gap between the wall and the door. Within seconds, the stones were sealed back in place as firmly as if they had never been taken out of the wall.

Breaking into a run, the four took off down the street, the angry cries of the mob fading behind them.

“Drop that staff and the four of us will go someplace nice and quiet,” sneered the hunter.

Chapter Six

In order to confuse the sneak, they headed back along Wolf River and hunted up a small boat. Tinker, who had never shown a moment's fear up to that point, was surprisingly skittish about getting aboard. "They move so much," he said apologetically, while reluctantly edging one foot at a time into the skiff. When John felt it shift and settle deep under Tinker's weight, he understood why Tinker was so reluctant.

Instead of crossing the river, which seemed like the logical thing to do, they doubled back toward the docks of Krovesport, skirting the shore in the rosy twilight, making their way to the docks from the water. As it grew dark, John was able to use the shadows to his advantage, and they managed to make it safely under one of the big piers, where they tied the boat off to one of the pilings and stopped to talk quietly and decide their next move.

John argued that he was the one who should go up onto the docks and scout for food and information.

Tinker was absolutely out, as he was the most easily recognized one of the bunch. And while John could use the *unlight* in a pinch if he needed to, he couldn't use it on behalf of Merridi or Lafe if they got more than a few yards away.

After some more arguing, which John knew he would win, they moved the skiff further under the pier. They would be losing the concealment of the *unlight* while John was gone, and Lafe didn't want to make it any easier for them to be spotted. Once that was taken care of, John snuck out of the boat and climbed the metal rungs of the big piling they were tied to, making his way to the beams that supported the pier, and from there up the vertical side of the plank-walk to the pier proper.

With the help of his *unlight*, John was more concerned about falling than he was about being spotted. It was full dark, with only the thinnest sliver of the new Zard moon above the horizon, and he was confident of his ability to conceal himself in the deep shadows. But the metal climbing rungs were cold and slick with salt water, and he was weighted with his damp cloak and the goldenrod staff slung across his back.

When he finally reached the safety of the boardwalk, he collapsed against a piling and tried to breathe through his mouth, so his panting breath wouldn't be heard by the few passersby. There was nothing he could do about the thundering of his heart.

As he sat, he realized that even though there was little activity, the docks were alive with noise. The huge ships rubbed restlessly against their moorings, as if they were eager seahorses who couldn't wait to race across the waves again; the wooden planks creaked irritably, and voices calling across the water echoed until it was difficult to determine where they were coming from.

Gathering his resolve, he stood up and went in search of information. And food. Thinking of Tinker, he sighed. A *lot* of food.

John scouted futilely for dock hands discussing the schedule of ships departing the docks soon. Unfortunately, the few wharf rats scattered about seemed more inclined to talk about taverns and women and gold than about who was going where and when. After an hour of unsuccessful eavesdropping, John decided to take a chance.

During several circuits of the docks, he had noticed a single light burning in a small, office-like room on the ground floor of *The Bilge Hole*, a grimy tavern that smelled a lot like its namesake. A small wooden sign hung above the office door, "Rhubarb Shipping." At the desk John could see through the single window a large man, well into his thirties by appearance. He was sitting at a desk decorated with a big blue puffball. The man looked a little rough and gruff, with clothes more like a pirate's than an officer's, but his face was kindly and he just *looked* like someone who could be trusted – not to ask too many questions, not to back out on a deal, not to talk.

Grabbing his courage in both hands, John quelled

the *unlight* and swallowed. Stepping forward, he knocked on the door.

A gruff voice called, "come in." John slipped through the heavy wooden door, swinging it shut behind him.

"I'm looking for berth on a ship," said John. "Do you deal with passengers?"

There was a moment of silence as the man behind the desk inspected John with his one good eye. The other was covered by a black patch. Then he put down his pen and leaned forward, smiling slightly, holding out a hand for John to shake. "I'm Captain Tom Rhubarb, and I do, on occasion, provide passage to a worthy customer. Who would you be?"

At that moment, the big blue puffball moved, revealing huge silly eyes and a bird-like beak.

The captain noticed John's surprise and grinned. "Oh, he won't hurt you, lad. He's a trobble. Cute little bugger, eh?"

"Like a pet?" asked John.

"Wouldn't do without one, any time of the day or night," replied the captain. "Friendly chappies, good company, always ready to listen, and don't talk your ear off like some people do."

John held out his hand, and the trobble waddled across the desk to see if there was anything interesting in there. When it realized he had no food, it turned its big, winsome eyes on him and chirruped inquiringly.

Captain Rhubarb reached obligingly into a bowl and produced a small treat for John to feed the trobble.

Once that was done, the captain turned back to business. "Now, what did you say your name was?"

"I'm Viz," said John, thinking fast. "Viz Spectrum." Captain Rhubarb held out his hand and they shook solemnly.

"You look too young to be an assassin out for my blood, and too clean-cut to be lookin' for work as a pi— as a sailor," the Captain said, "so I guess you *must* be looking for passage."

John shrugged. "I'm not an assassin or a sailor. And I'm not *that* young. Just small for my age. I'm looking for a ship out of here as soon as possible, as long as it's going where I need to go."

"And where would that be, laddie?"

"Deren. Do you know of any ships going to Deren in the near future?"

"Deren? Now, I must say that surprises me. Most folk that have been looking for a berth are either trying to get to the dragon wars, or further away from them. But you, you want to head out in a different direction altogether. Why is that, if I may ask ye?"

"I'm interested in becoming a scholar," said John. "I'm seeking passage to the School of Thought."

The Captain looked genuinely surprised. "You don't look much like a scholar, either, if I may say so. You sure about that?"

"Sure," said John firmly.

"Well, there's a ship leaving tomorrow I could get you on, but it's a trade ship, so it's got some tradin' to do on its way. Leaves soon, but will take awhile to get there, if you get my drift."

"Tomorrow?" John couldn't believe the good news.

"Aye, with passage charge of five gold coins. Ten if you want to share in the sailors' mess."

"Ten gold coins?" John squeaked, his voice rising with his disappointment.

"Aye. 'Tis expensive to cruise the oceans, laddie. Did ye think it would be some piddling amount?"

"Well, not as much as that," said John. He had been thinking that if he could get a legitimate berth, the others would have an easier time of hiding. So much for that plan.

"Of course, we do have an economy package," said the Captain, watching John's face.

"What's that?"

"Join the crew, Viz. Same great ocean views, same good, wholesome food, plus lots of fresh air and some good healthy exercise. Put some meat on those bones! What do you say?"

Slowly John nodded. He couldn't see any other way.

"I'll be with you on-board for a short hop – I've got to get back to me home port of Lolosia."

John looked around the office. "Isn't this where you're from?"

"Nah, laddie. Just a small office I keep here for when I'm in town. We'll leave tomorrow morning at dawn. Look for the *Blinkin' Mermaid*, and don't be late." The captain stood up and they shook hands again, then John departed to see if he could scare up a meal for his comrades before returning to tell them the news.

"You're going to be crewing on a trade ship?" asked

Lafe, incredulous, as they wolfed down the meat pies and cider John had stolen from the kitchen of *The Splintery Bench*, a tavern just a few blocks over.

"I know, pretty amazing, huh?" said John, proud of himself. "It will give me more access to the ship and the crew, and I won't have to sneak around so much to stay on top of what's happening."

"The rest of us still have to get on board, though," said Merridi.

"And find a place to hide," added Tinker. "a *big* place."

Lafe nodded agreement, mouth full. "Soon as we finish eating," he said after swallowing, spraying crumbs everywhere.

"Yeah," added John, "we're sailing at dawn. The sooner, the better."

The Zard moon had set and the second moon had not yet popped up when they located the *Blinkin' Mermaid*. They crept up the gangplank cautiously, almost giving themselves away when a dockworker bumped into Tinker while carrying a large box on board.

"Hey," he cried, bobbling the heavy box. "Look where you're going! This weighs like a stone!"

"Sorry," muttered Tinker apologetically, realizing the man couldn't see him – or *not* see him, in the *unlight* – over the top of the box.

"That's better," said the man, hurrying by. "Next time, look where you're going."

"*Suns*," said John when he was gone, "that was a close one!"

Merridi giggled, more from nerves than amusement, and John shushed her. He had learned the lesson of the library well. The *unlight* did not blanket sound. Even if they could not be seen, they could still be heard. Silently, they made their way down to the hold to look for a hiding place.

As a trading ship, the *Blinkin' Mermaid*'s hold was large, and the captain was anticipating they would pick up more cargo as they went. Consequently, the hold was no more than halfway full. It wasn't hard at all, thanks to Tinker's immense strength, to rearrange a few boxes and make themselves a cozy hiding spot behind the main portion of the goods stored in the hold.

With his friends settled, John went back up top to announce his presence and officially join the crew.

To keep from arousing suspicion, he snuck back down the gangplank into the street and around the corner. When he was sure no one was looking, he quelled the *unlight* and shoved his staff down into his belt, where it was hidden by his cloak. He was just about to get back on to the gangplank when he spotted Captain Rhubarb, standing outside his office door, deep in conversation with a cloaked figure. Moving cautiously forward, John was able to get a look at the man's profile.

Suns! It was Barstow, the hunter who was after Merridi.

John ducked behind a pile of crates and watched as the man leaned forward menacingly into Captain Rhubarb's face. Captain Rhubarb sneered and leaned back; Barstow hissed, but seemed to relent, snapping off a few more words, then stalking away angrily.

Captain Rhubarb stared after him for a long minute, then turned, shaking his head. He spied John, who had just emerged from behind the crates. "Ahoy there, laddie! Glad to see you decided to join us."

"Who was that?" asked John.

The Captain shrugged his broad shoulders. "Some madman, looking for dragons disguised as children. What kind of nonsense is that, do you think?"

John hesitated, not sure what the captain might have heard on the docks. Surely, he hadn't missed all the gossip, had he? "There was some crazy talk I heard about that, too, but it didn't make any sense. I never did figure out what it was about."

"There's always someone talking crazy in my experience," said the captain, setting a hand on John's shoulder. "Now, let's get you aboard and get you settled."

Getting you settled quickly turned out to be *getting you to work*, but John didn't mind. It felt good to have something to do besides worry. The *Blinkin' Mermaid* was a busy ship, and there was always something for a junior cabin boy to do. Scrubbing decks, peeling potatoes and helping the cook, repairing sails, polishing, cleaning, stacking, climbing – you name it, it needed to be done. One of the advantages of helping the cook was that it made it easier for John to get provisions for his friends, who were bored stiff in the hold.

One thing John had been surprised to learn was that Captain Rhubarb wasn't actually the captain of this particular voyage. That was Captain Frolgar, a gray-haired, one-legged, squinty-eyed sailor who swore he hadn't been on shore in a decade.

"Aye, 'tis not as often as I like that I get to captain one of my own ships anymore, Viz," said Captain Rhubarb when he'd introduced the new cabin boy to Captain Frolgar.

"But ye're captain of them all, and that's a grand thing," returned Frolgar, a little kissy-uppity for John's taste.

Still, while Frolgar wasn't Rhubarb, he seemed alright, and John had plenty to think about without pondering the differences between the two men.

Since the cabin boys shared a room with several berths in it and everybody took shifts in the rope beds, John frequently spent his free time in the hold with Lafe, Tinker, and Merridi discussing their plans, reading from *A Brief History of Magic*, or swapping tales from their pasts. Occasionally, John would run into Captain Rhubarb on deck, who was never too busy for a few words and to inquire as to John's progress as a sailor.

One night, Captain Rhubarb surprised John, who was out on the deck, smelling the cool night air. John had thought he was by himself, when a figure stepped out of the shadows and resolved itself into the familiar shape of the captain.

"Ahoy there, Viz! And how is me newest cabin boy this fine night?"

"Doing well, Captain Rhubarb. How about yourself?"

"Fine, laddie. There's no better time for a sailin' man than on the sea, no matter how profitable it may be for him to remain on land."

John felt a tug of sympathy for the captain. More than once he'd seen Rhubarb watching longingly as a crew member climbed the rigging or trimmed the sails, or even manned the great ship's wheel, only to be called into one meeting or another regarding the trade route, the cargo fees, or exchange rates – whatever those were.

"I like to come out top at night sometimes and look at the stars," John said, after some companionable silence.

"Aye," replied the captain. "We steer by those, you know. If you know your stars, you'll never be lost, Viz."

"I know some of the constellations," said John, pointing. "There's the Leaping Zard, and there's Lorithia's Well..."

"Ye're a smart laddie," said the captain. "Do you see that one over there, by the horizon?"

John looked in the direction the captain was pointing.

"It's the great dragon, Viz. See the great star that glows green? That's her great green eye. And there, her claws, and that curved line there – all the little stars? That marks her tail. She's a sign of wisdom and peace, the star masters say."

"A dragon? The sign of wisdom and peace?"

"Ah, you're on the human side of the dragon wars, eh, Viz? Well, not all dragons are evil. Just like humans, each dragon has its own destiny to pursue, and as likely it is to be a good path as a bad one, I suppose."

"I didn't know there was such as thing as a good dragon. I thought they were all evil."

"Every monster isn't an evil one, young Viz. 'Tis nothing on this world as simple as it looks. Remember that, as you make your way, Viz. Good advice, from a man who doesn't give much out."

"I will, Captain," said John. And he remained on deck for a long time, thinking about what the captain had said.

Much quicker than John expected, they arrived at Lolosia to drop off Captain Rhubarb and collect some additional wares for trade. They were sailing sleekly into the colorful port and John was readying the port-side ropes for tie-off, when he saw a sight that made his gut tighten. On the dock stood Barstow, the hunter, accompanied by a man John vaguely remembered from the mob in Krovesport. Between them coiled the tracking sneak.

John's mind froze, as the *Blinkin' Mermaid* sailed closer and closer to the man who had vowed to destroy Merridi and all her friends.

A hand on his shoulder made him jump, until he realized it belonged to Captain Rhubarb, who was eyeing their welcoming committee with narrowed eyes. "That crazy land-lubber again! I knew it! He's working for the port authority, I'll bet my cutlass on it! Don't they know I'm an honest businessman now? Does he think he's gonna use that trackin' sneak to search my cargo for contraband? He's got another thing coming! Grab one of those ten-inch cannon balls, laddie, quick-like."

While John did as he was bid, Captain Rhubarb was manning the nearest cannon, bringing it to bear on the dock, primed and ready for the cannon ball John staggered over with. No sooner was the ball loaded than Captain Rhubarb pulled his flint striker and lit the fuse. Even as the two men at the dock realized what the Captain's intentions were and attempted to fling themselves out of the way, there was a huge explosion of sound and the ball was rocketing through the air.

It landed right where Barstow and his companion had been standing, and the two men went flying through the air. Barstow crashed – *hard* – into a pile of crates. The other man went straight over the breakwater and into the sea. The tracking sneak, which for all its powers was oblivious to the connection between the actions of a man on a faraway boat and its own precious self, had not even tried to dodge. Its splattered remains decorated the pier from one end to the other.

As John gaped, Captain Rhubarb let out a lusty victory yell, then picked John up for a bone-crunching jig. "That'll teach that nosey landlubber to keep his sneaks away from my cargo!"

John cast another look at Barstow, who hadn't moved from his crumpled position on top of the crates that had broken his fall. He grinned. "Aye, aye Captain!"

The crew seemed to see nothing unusual about Captain Rhubarb shooting off a cannon at someone with a sneak waiting on the dock for the *Blinkin' Mermaid*. Under the guise of offering a helpful hand to a drunken sailor, a couple of the men hustled a considerably addled Barstow away from the docks as the *Blinkin' Mermaid*'s crew hustled their new cargo up the gangplank and made ready to set sail in record time.

When the men who had stiff-armed Barstow away returned to report to Captain Rhubarb, John slipped close enough to overhear the conversation. "We got him stowed up in a room at Molly's, and Doc Boombatz gave him a little something for that concussion that will keep him under till the *Mermaid*'s back underway." The sailor grinned in a way that made John glad he didn't have to take whatever medicine Doc Boombatz had given Barstow.

"We fished the other one out of the drink," the sailor continued, "but all he cared about was his stinkin' sneak. We took him to the magistrate to file a complaint like he asked for, and Judge Jonah gave him seven days for bringing an unlicensed sneak into a populated area. Oh, and the judge says he'll give you the bill for the dock when you bring him those cigars he asked for."

There was a round of laughter at that, and John slipped away to let his friends know that, for the present, they were still safe.

The tide turned the next morning a few minutes

after the sun came up, and the *Blinkin' Mermaid* sped away, sails proudly unfurled. Life aboard the ship settled into a peaceful, if busy, routine for John. In the hold, Tinker, Lafe, and Merridi struggled to contain their growing restlessness, and once they were well away from dry land, John took to slipping one of them out every night under cover of his *unlight* so they could get some fresh air and look at the stars.

They headed onward across calm seas toward Bridgetown and their first port of call. They were laying over for two nights, and against John's better judgment, he agreed to help Merridi, Lafe, and Tinker sneak off the ship so they could enjoy a couple of days of sunshine and freedom before stowing back away in the cargo hold.

Everything went well until it was time to get everyone back on board, when once again there was an incident involving a crew member being inadvertently touched by one of the Corrs making their stealthy way back into the hold.

This time, however, the crewman wasn't willing to blame it on a clumsy, but unseen fellow sailor. Instead, he dropped the big box he was carrying to peer around the shadowy space fearfully.

"Who's there?" He called out, voice shaking. John and the other Corrs watched in silence, not sure what to do.

When there was no reply, the sailor abandoned his box, and fled back the way he had come. Seconds later came the clanging bell that announced the ship was underway. There was a lurch, and the groan of wood sliding against wood, and then the *Blinkin' Mermaid* slid away from the dock and back to open waters.

John could feel Merridi shiver against him. They were so close! Deren and freedom were just days away. Without thinking, he reached out a comforting hand. "I'll go up top and see what's happening," he whispered. He could feel her nod. Then he turned to go topside, while his shaken companions returned to their hiding place.

He found most of the crew gathered in the galley, with more arriving by the minute.

"The hold is haunted, I swear," cried the man that Lafe had accidentally bumped into. "Some awful spirit reached out and grabbed me in the dark!"

"Aye," said another man. "I was down right after we left Krovesport, and heard voices speaking, clear as I can hear Belchy right now. But when I went lookin' t'weren't no one there."

"And food's been disappearin' from the galley," chimed in one of the cook's assistants.

"My bed got short-sheeted last week," said someone from the back of the crowd.

Everyone turned to look at him.

"Just sayin'," he muttered. They all turned back.

"You fools," cried Captain Frolgar, who was pushing his way through the crowd. "That's not haunts! That's stowaways! What use would haunts have for food from the galley, you great lump of lubbers? Grab a cutlass and follow me."

He pulled his own cutlass from its sheath and rushed from the galley, followed by his crew.

In the hold, they lit torches and scoured the space between crates, an elaborate maze that crawled with shadows. John headed off in a different direction and raced to get to his friends before the crew did, covering them with *unlight* when he arrived. They picked a stealthy path through the crates away from the searchers, and John felt his heart slide into his feet as a cry of discovery went up - their hiding place had been found.

Once the crew had confirmed that it was live stowaways and not undead haunts they faced, the search was more enthusiastic.

Before long, they were cornered. John could hear the searchers getting closer by the second. His heart was loud in his ears.

"John," whispered Lafe urgently. "Find us!"

"What?

"It's our best chance! Kill the shadow light, and find us. If they find us all together, you'll just get thrown in the brig, too. If you find us, you'll still be free. At least you'll be able to help us then. If you're in the brig, too, we're lost."

John looked at Merridi and Tinker, who nodded agreement.

Reluctantly acknowledging the wisdom of Lafe's statement, John quelled the *unlight*.

"Here!" he called. "I found them!"

The call was quickly taken up by the rest of the crew, "It's Viz! Viz found them!" and in an eye blink, the stowaways were surrounded. Unceremoniously, they were led away to the brig, as Captain Frolgar clapped John on the back in congratulations. "Good job there, young Viz! There'll be something extra for you in it when we dock, rest assured!"

"Great," said John weakly. "What are you going to

do to them?"

"What we always do to stowaways," said Captain Frolgar, urging John forward and out of the hold. "What they hate the most."

"What's that?"

"Why, we take 'em right back where they came from. This bunch will end up being delivered right back to the magistrate at Krovesport."

John knew he and the others could have fought going to the brig and probably won, but he didn't feel like fighting any more.

Chapter Seven

Captain Frolgar and the rest of the crew were still unaware of John's connection to the prisoners, so he managed to use the *unlight* to sneak down and visit them when he could manage it. He was afraid to try and sneak any more food out of the kitchen but, as near as he could tell, they were getting the same provisions he was, so it didn't really matter anymore. He would have released them, but on board the ship there was no place for them to go.

There were crew assigned to bring down the food and take away the trays but, other than that, they were left mostly on their own. The key to their cells hung prominently on a big iron ring just out of reach on one of the walls. John suggested letting them out, but Lafe shrugged. "We're in the middle of the sea. That's why they're not guarding us closer. Where do we have to go?"

Made sense. "I can set you free when we get to Paxia. We can slip away then. We can find a ship from

Paxia to Deren pretty easy, I bet."

In a big ship like the *Blinkin' Mermaid*, with all its sails unfurled, the distance between Paxia and Deren was a skip across a puddle compared to how far they had already come.

Tinker, his usual calm self, retreated into a contemplative state that seemed almost monk-like, he was so serene. "Like Lafe said, nothing we can do until we get to land anyway. Why fight it?"

Merridi was the one who had the hardest time with being locked up. She jittered and paced, and then spent hours standing with her face pressed to the tiny porthole that her cell contained.

John could empathize, even though he didn't want to; he'd been locked up for a few weeks, and a black cloud of depression had nearly paralyzed him. According to her own story, Merridi had been locked up for months in a human-cage by her own people. He wondered if the time she spent in human form seemed like being in a cage to her. Dragons were so … big. And free.

It occurred to him that if she really wanted to, she could break out of the puny cell any time and force the crew to take her where she wanted to go.

"Merridi," he called softly.

She turned from the porthole to look at him, green eyes dull. "What?"

"How come you don't just bust out of here and … I don't know … eat people until they take you to Deren or something?"

Something sparked briefly in her eyes. "I don't

know, John, why don't you just shoot light beams at people until they bow to your will?"

"I can't do that. It's not right, forcing people just because I can. I don't like bullies."

Her eyes flashed again. "I don't either." And she turned her back on him, going back to her tiny view of the endless sea from her porthole.

They were due to arrive at the island of Paxia within the next day or so, and the sun was already preparing to slip below the horizon. John was sitting in the brig, talking quietly with his friends, when there was a horrible clanging noise from on deck. They all jumped to their feet as a tumultuous shouting began. John looked at Lafe uncertainly. He wanted to go find out what was going on, but if there was trouble, he wanted to be with his friends. "Go," said Lafe. "Stay undercover and come back to tell us what's going on. Take care of yourself – if anything happens to you, we're all blunted!"

John nodded and sped topside, where he emerged into chaos. Off the starboard bow, he could see a dark ship with a high, curled prow and ash-gray sails, bristling with cannon. The cannon were pointed right at the *Blinkin' Mermaid*.

Sailors were rushing past him in both directions, cursing and shouting orders, as they armed themselves with cutlasses and pistols. He caught the words, "Black

Raiders!" several times, but had no idea what that meant. Several smaller boats from the dark ship had already arrived at side of the *Blinkin' Mermaid*, and the raiders these boats carried were swarming up and over the sides of it. The raiders presented a dreadful front, dressed in dark colors and great, horned helmets, blades clenched between pointed yellow teeth.

One raider had topped the railing right in front of John, who was sure he would be skewered immediately, forgetting that he was hidden by the *unlight*. Instead, the raider ran right by him, thrusting his sword at one of John's shipmates. Sticking out his staff, John tripped the raider and the seaman John saved – who had been quaking in his boots a minute before – pounced on his attacker with glee.

Not waiting to see what else might happen, John raced back down to the brig.

"We're being attacked! We've been boarded by a bunch of raiders from a big, dark ship and everybody's fighting everywhere!"

"Grab the keys! Get us out of here, John! If they decide to scuttle the ship, we'll be doomed!"

John looked around frantically, then spotted the keys hanging from their habitual spot just out of reach of anyone closed inside one of the cells. Because they were at sea, and the only real escape was to jump into the water and swim for it, security was pretty casual. John grabbed the keys and unlocked the cell doors with urgent hands.

He raced back up to the deck, his companions right behind him, and nearly ran in to Captain Frolgar, who looked at John, then at the prisoners arrayed behind them. To John's surprise, he clapped a hand on John's shoulder. "Good thinkin' laddie! We can use a good, strong troll on our side. These raiders don't take no prisoners, you three, so if you want to live, your only hope is to throw in with us." So saying, he snatched a mace from hands of a fallen crewman and tossed it to Tinker, and lunged off in pursuit of one of the dark raiders.

The four of them stayed as close together as they could, John using the *unlight* to keep them as safe as possible, while plying his staff to knock down – or knock out – any raiders that came within reach. Tinker swung his mace with abandon and when Lafe snatched up a discarded sword, he proved that knew more about blades than just how to hit a target with a short knife. He'd sent half a dozen raiders scrambling back over the railing and diving into the sea to escape his blade. Merridi was doing pretty well also, using a peculiar kind of unarmed combat that involved both her feet and her hands to topple several raiders.

The first time she bested one of the deadly raiders, Merridi looked at John, who was regarding her with open astonishment and smiled. "No place to carry a weapon when my people are in dragon form! We learn how to fight like this so we're prepared – no matter what."

John nodded, then stuck out his staff as another hapless raider went rushing by. The raider tripped and cursed, but before he could get back to his feet Tinker clubbed him with the mace, and he went down on the deck, snoring like a baby.

Another raider ran up to take the place of his fallen comrade; Merridi started the smooth motion that would end with her booted foot on the raider's ear, but a gesture from Lafe stopped her.

"Dad?"

"What? Who said that?" said the raider in confusion, eyes darting left and right.

At a look from Lafe, John quelled the *unlight* so that Lafe could be seen by the frightening looking man standing in front of them. When he appeared, the raider rubbed his eyes, then stepped forward, an incredulous look on his face.

"Lafe? Son? What are you doing here?"

"What the *shiv* are you doing here, Dad? You're supposed to be at Smoke Mountain, fighting in the dragon wars!"

His father looked embarrassed. "I went down there, but couldn't get signed on, Lafe. Bad shoulder. You know how it goes. But there was another outfit takin' on men, and well, one thing led to another, and here I am! Didn't expect you to find out, though."

Lafe shook his head. "Dad, you're fighting on the side of the *bad* guys!"

"Man's gotta make a living. And what are you doing here, anyway?"

"Taking a sea voyage with my friends. You left me behind anyway. What's it to you?"

Lafe's father winced. "We been through that, Lafe. I left you there to keep you safe. How did I know you were gonna take off and go sailing and end up on a ship attacked by … me? You better come with me now, son. I'll get you back aboard the *Death Raider*, and we'll fix it somehow. Your mates here are pretty much finished. Looks like it's all over but the shoutin', to tell you the truth."

They all turned to glance around the deck, and it was obvious Lafe's father was telling the truth. The crewmen of the *Blinkin' Mermaid* had fought valiantly, but they were sorely outnumbered, and already many of them were being rounded up to walk the plank.

"What about my friends?" asked Lafe.

"Where are they?" asked his dad. "Sure they haven't already been thrown into the drink?"

Lafe gestured, and John quelled the *unlight*. He, Tinker, and Merridi stepped forward so that Lafe's father could see them.

"Huh! This appearing, disappearing trick you got going is something, Lafe. But there's no way I can get the captain to take on four of ya's. I'm sorry, Lafe, but your friends are gonna have to take their chances in the briny deeps. Captain says he wants this ship and everything on it, with no prisoners."

"Dad, I can't leave them here!"

Lafe's dad looked around nervously. "Sure you can, son, and you better step on it, too. Say goodbye, and let's get while the gettin's good!"

Lafe looked at his father, then at his friends, sorrow in his face. John didn't blame him for leaving. The battle was just about over, and it wasn't the crew of the *Blinkin' Mermaid* that had won.

"Sorry, Dad. I can't go."

"What?" said his dad.

"What?" said John.

Tinker grinned. "I knew it!"

"I'm not leaving my friends. But you better step back if you don't want to get crushed, because the dragon and the mage are about to go all doom on your butts!" Lafe looked pointedly at Merridi and John. John knew he was right. He had no idea how far they were from land, but he had no desire to try and swim for it from wherever they were. He couldn't even see land from where they were, and would have had no idea what direction to swim in. Plus, he was pretty sure trolls were lousy swimmers. About dragons, he had no idea whatsoever.

"Lafe, quit funning around and get in the boat, son. I'll be there as soon as we make the rest of these seadogs walk the plank."

"John, will you help my father off our ship, please?"

"Are you sure?"

"Yes," said Lafe firmly. "Merridi, time to do your thing, too."

Reluctantly, John pointed his staff at Lafe's dad, and let the power flow. At his side, he could feel Merridi starting her change.

The ball of light flew from John's staff and struck Lafe's dad square in the chest. The last thing John saw of him was the surprised look on his face as he went flying through the air and over the side of the *Mermaid*'s railing. John looked over the side of the ship. In the sea, he could make out Lafe's father bobbing to the surface and striking out toward one of the smaller raider boats ringing the *Mermaid*.

John turned back to Lafe. "He's okay. He's almost to one of the raider's small boats."

Then he looked up. Way up. At the top of a long, slender, scaled neck, Merridi's green eyes looked out at him from a dragon's face. He wondered if she was really as loyal as she said she was. If she really felt the same way about them all when she was a dragon that she did when she was in human form. Then she winked at him.

Merridi lifted up her head and let out a challenging roar. The clanging of blade on blade and the shouts and curses of fighting men ceased.

"A dragon! There's a *sharkin'* dragon on board!"

Several of the raiders dived overboard without any further discussion. Unfortunately, so did several of the *Mermaid*'s crew, having no idea which side the dragon was on.

They had just about gotten it sorted out, however, when there was a dull "boom!" and a shiver ran through the *Mermaid*.

"Cannon!" bellowed Lafe. "They've armed the cannon!"

"John! Use your light! Quick!"

John had not yet tried his focused light beam on a target so far away but, summoning everything he had, he poured it into his staff, which flared so brightly it burned his hand. He didn't let go though, pointing the stone at the cannon on the *Death Raider*. They already had two more cannon loaded with shot, and another half a dozen that they were in the process of pulling the grappling hooks from.

The beam of light ran straight and true and sweet, a dozen perfect spheres of light, each one striking an open cannon mouth as he swung his staff, melting the heavy iron barrels on contact.

The rest of the raiders on board looked at John, still holding his flaring staff. Then they looked at the *Death Raider*, whose melted cannons were giving off a dark smoke.

As one, they jumped over railing of the ship in all directions.

John bit his lip and redirected his staff so that the light formed a tight beam. Under Lafe's approving eye, he scorched the words "The Corrs Were Here!" across the hull in ten-foot-high letters.

Done, he turned to his companions with a grin on his face. "Teach them to mess with us!"

They watched for a moment, as the raiders who were scattered in the water raced to get back to their ship, which was already hoisting sail to turn and turn. Then they got busy fishing the rest of the *Mermaid*'s crew out of the sea.

Soon, the crew of the *Blinkin' Mermaid* was gathered in the galley, most of them, in John's opinion, only benefiting from a dip in the sea. There were several who had taken some pretty serious knocks on the head, and one more with a broken arm, but all in all they had faired pretty well. Three of the crew were missing entirely, but another sailor reported they'd been seen swimming for the *Death Raider*. Whether they were just confused or actually trying to join up with the raiders, no one was sure, but they had looked like they were okay as they dog-paddled away from the *Mermaid*.

Too soon, the conversation got around to their miraculous salvation by a scarlet dragon and a light mage.

Merridi had returned to her human form, and was sitting with her shoulders curled, trying to make herself as small and harmless looking as possible, but Captain Frolgar didn't look convinced. Once he had seen to the welfare of his crew, he completed the head count, and had the remaining raiders thrown in the brig or overboard – if they could swim. Then he turned his attention to his former stowaways, trying to make themselves as inconspicuous as possible.

"So," began the captain, "I hear that it's you three – and you, Viz, that we owe our victory to."

John nodded cautiously.

"I also hear that the girl is actually a dragon in disguise, and you yourself are by way of bein' a mage."

'I … ah … yeah," said John, unable to think of anything to say to refute that.

"Based on my keen wits and powers of observation, I'm guessing that the four of you have known each other since before ye got aboard my ship.'

More nodding. John felt miserable as all eyes in the galley turned his way.

"Which means you were aiding and abetting these

stowaways the whole time."

There was some muttering from the crew. Captain Frolgar held up a hand and the muttering stopped.

"On the other hand, the bunch of ye stopped the *Blinkin' Mermaid* from being overrun by raiders and the crew from all being thrown in the drink.'

"Saw 'em do it with me own eyes!" called someone from the back, and John thought it was one of the other cabin boys.

The captain paced slowly around them, stopping behind Tinker, who was as tall sitting as the feisty captain was standing up. Captain Frolgar paused, gazing at the back of Tinker's head for a moment, then shook his own and moved on.

"Now, ye know we have a strict 'no stowaways' policy aboard the *Mermaid*. As a matter of fact, our original plan was to return these young rascals to Krovesport. But my thinkin's somewhat changed on that matter. We owe 'em something here, and that's a fact."

There were a few shouts of support for this sentiment from the crowd.

But there was something else, too, something darker, that John couldn't quite put his finger on, until he heard someone mutter, "I ain't sailin' with no dragon!"

There it was. Regardless of how grateful the crew was about not being pitched headfirst into the briny deep by the raiders, there *was* a dragon war going on, and human sentiment was running high – and not in favor of the dragons.

He was on his feet before he realized what he was

doing. "What are you talking about? She saved your lives!"

Captain Frolgar put his hand on John's shoulder, but John shook it off. "You think that because one dragon has started a war that means that all dragons are blood-thirsty maniacs? You're wrong. I know this dragon. And she's nothing like that. Nothing at all. And if you're too stupid to see that, then *sparks* to the lot of you."

He had forgotten his staff. His hands were clenched into fists, ready to punch the first person who said so much as a word against Merridi.

He realized that Lafe was regarding him with open-mouthed astonishment, while Merridi— was she going to cry? *Suns!* He sat back down, but kept his chin up, just in case anyone wanted to argue the point.

"Viz, we all realize what yer friend did for us today. What all of ye did today. But some have more trouble than others actually helping a creature when we humans are at war with her kind. And bein' as these folks are me crew, I have to take their feelin's on the subject into account, too."

Captain Frolgar stood and looked in the faces of his men for a long minute, then sighed and turned back to John and his friends.

"We won't take you back to Krovesport, if that's what yer worried about."

John looked up at him, surprised.

"But … we ain't taken ye no further, either."

"I don't get it," said John. "You're gonna put us overboard after all this?"

"No, lad, nothing so cruel as that."

"They're going to maroon us," said Lafe in a harsh voice, narrowed eyes on the captain's face.

Captain Frolgar flushed and looked away.

"Marooned? I don't get it." said John.

"That's because you're a farmer's kid," said Lafe. "It's what they do when they don't want to kill you, but they want to make sure you don't cause any more trouble to anyone – maybe permanently. They stick you on an uninhabited island with a few supplies, and leave you there to live or die by your wits."

"That's horrible!" said Merridi.

"We're not gonna stick you on there with a jar of peaches and four spoons," said Captain Frolgar, face turning red. "But the crew won't put up with ye goin' any further with us, and I won't take ye back. That's a compromise, ain't it?"

"Yeah, what a choice. Jail or being stranded in the middle of the sea," said Lafe bitterly.

From the crew came the unmistakable sound of several pistols being cocked.

"Take it or leave it, it's the best offer yer gonna get," said the captain. "Unless you'd rather walk the plank. We won't have a dragon on the *Blinkin' Mermaid*."

John held up a hand, and several of the closest members of the crew ducked. Hastily, he put his hand back down.

"It's okay," he said. "We won't try to force you in to anything you don't want to do. Just give us enough supplies to make a go of it, leave us somewhere with a few signs of life, okay?"

"That's a promise, Viz. Now, off to the brig with ye."

It occurred to John that he and the others could have fought going to the brig – and probably won, but he didn't feel like fighting any more, and the others looked pretty miserable, too. Even Lafe, who usually had a comeback for anything, and Tinker, who was one of the most even-tempered people John had ever met. So he kept his mouth shut and let himself be led away along with his friends, figuring if things didn't go well, he could always blast a hole in the hull and they could make their escape in the sea, no worse off than they would have been if they'd been forced to walk the plank. The other option was to blast down the cell door and fight their way through the crew, but that didn't have much more appeal than going for a long swim in salty water.

They weren't in the brig long, though. Due to the raiders, the captain and crew had decided to vacate the area of the sea where the battle had occurred without stopping at Paxia. They were on a course due east when they stumbled across a narrow spit of land lush with foliage and with a deep-enough bay for the *Blinkin' Mermaid* to anchor comfortably.

The captives were hastily removed from the brig and rowed ashore, with several barrels of water, a pistol with a supply of powder and shot, and two cases of provisions. The captain came with them to see them safely set on shore.

"There's fresh water here, or there wouldn't be so much greenery," the captain observed. "And ye got fruit trees, and I made sure to put in some fishin' hooks and line. You'll do fine. Keep a fire goin', nice and smoky, and some poor sap will stop and pick you up, right enough. Sorry I am I couldn't help ye more, but a crew's a temperamental beastie, never more than a few whiskers away from mutiny, and they was already shook by the raiders. Thanks for all yer help, and may Neso bless and keep ye all."

"Who's Neso?" asked Tinker.

"Lady of the waters, young fella," replied the captain, removing his hat for an instant, then clapping it back on his head.

"Now, mateys, look spritely there," called out the captain to the sailors who had accompanied them, "and lets get these provisions unloaded. I want to be back on the ship and well away before the tide turns!"

He solemnly shook their hands as the provisions were placed on the beach, then hopped spryly back into the boat that would carry him back to the *Blinkin' Mermaid*. John and the others watched silently until the captain was back aboard the Mermaid, the ship itself was making a hasty retreat back to open seas.

Lafe sighed and threw himself down on the shore. "Well," he said, shading his eyes with his hand and looking up at the rest of them. "Any of you Corrs know how to build a boat?"

Chapter Eight

The first clue they had that the island wasn't uninhabited was the music.

It started as a barely audible flutter of pipes, almost like the wind through reeds. Merridi heard it first, head lifted as if seeking the source of the sound just as it crossed John's ears. John saw her stiffen as she oriented on it. He saw Tinker react, then last of all Lafe, who looked mildly alarmed at the idea of music pouring out of the dense jungle at their backs.

John looked at him, unsure what to think. "Is that *somebody* making that sound, or *something*?"

"I don't know," said Lafe, scrambling to his feet, "but I don't think we should wait around here in the open to find out. Come on, Tinker, grab those boxes, let's get some cover. Could just be some stupid bird or something, but I'd like to see the noisemaker before the noisemaker sees *us*."

They grabbed their gear and headed for the tree line,

which began a few hundred feet from the shore.

Merridi seemed half entranced, her fingers clumsy as she grabbed her things, head moving slightly in rhythm to what was definitely identifiable now as music.

Finding cover between the thick brush and the low-hanging branches of the trees wasn't too hard. John spread a little *unlight* to make their hiding place even more secure. Then they settled in to wait and see what would happen.

For a long while, there was nothing but the music. After the sun had moved a good fist's width across the sky, Lafe sighed. "If there's got to be music, at least it could be good music. This sounds like something my Aunt Gessie would go to sleep by."

John nodded and felt his thoughts drifting. It did have a rather hypnotic effect, chord after chord after chord. But there was something discordant under the surface, and he fretted as he tried to figure it out. Dark clouds rolled across the sky, and he struggled to rouse himself before they were drowned in a torrent of rain.

John's eyes popped open. The music was as pretty as it had been all along. The sun filtered down in pretty patterns through the bright green leaves overhead. He squinted up at the sky and was surprised at how much time had passed. He had looked up when Lafe spoke – surely it hadn't been that long ago?

He shook his head to clear it, still feeling chilled from the cold rain that hadn't fallen. "I must have nodded off without realizing it," he said. "You guys?"

He looked at his comrades. Lafe was snoozing, eyes shaded from the sun by the covering fronds of the tree they were under. Tinker appeared entranced by the music, nodding his head rhythmically, much as Merridi had when they first heard it.

Merridi was standing several feet away, head and shoulders bobbing sinuously, her entire body straining toward the source of the music. "Merridi!" hissed John.

"Merridi, what are you doing?" A chill ran down his spine when she turned and looked over her shoulder at him, a strange, fervent glaze in her eyes. Even as she looked back, she took another step toward the source of the music.

"Hey," said John, scrambling to his feet and reaching for her.

She took another step, and made a small, helpless sound. He tried to tug her back, and it was like she was being held in place with iron bars. He couldn't budge her an inch. She took another step forward.

Tinker stood up, and John shot him a grateful look, then realized that the same strange sheen was in his eyes, as well. Tinker was as much under the spell of the music as Merridi was.

"Lafe!" John shouted, too panicked to worry about being overheard.

Slowly, Lafe opened his eyes and looked at John from under heavy lids. "John, I don't feel so good. I … do you hear that music?"

"Of course I do," snapped out John, exasperated. "And it's doing something weird to Merridi and Tinker—"

Without warning, he was lifted off his feet. In a single-minded effort to follow Merridi, Tinker had simply picked John up and moved him out of the way.

As John watched, horrified, Merridi took two more steps and disappeared behind a curtain of thick foliage, Tinker right behind her.

He looked back for Lafe, who was beginning to bob his head in a way creepily similar to Merridi and Tinker. John grabbed his arm and tried to pull him back, but Lafe shook him off without a backward glance and walked off in the same direction as the others.

John grabbed his staff. He could feel the music pulling at him if he listened, and the feeling in the pit of his stomach told him this wasn't going to be a good thing. He looked around their small clearing for something – anything that could help. There was a glint of silvery light where Lafe had been sitting, back to the flour sack. John picked up the knife and cut a strip of cloth from the bag. Flour spilled out on the ground, but he didn't care. Cutting off pieces of the cloth with the knife, he rolled up two compact plugs and stuffed them into his ears. He stuffed the rest of the cloth in a pocket, in case he had the chance to make some for his friends.

Magic staff, knife, and earplugs. Check. He was as prepared as he knew how to be. At a lope, he took off after his friends.

It wasn't hard to follow Tinker's path through the jungle. The guy was half-troll, after all. John ran along the trail, grateful that his big friend had cleared the way of all obstacles simply by muscling through them where other people would be compelled to duck, or wiggle or detour. John marveled at how far they'd gone in the few minutes it had taken him to make the earplugs. He wondered if they were speeding up as they approached the apparently irresistible source of the music.

Finally the jungle started to thin out, and John made himself stop in his panicked chase long enough to call up some *unlight* to cloak himself in. He could see more than a few feet in front of him now, and realized that he was almost at the base of a huge mountain that looked entirely made of some forbidding black rock. Not a single leaf or blade of grass clung to its sullen exterior. Tinker's big tracks, accompanied by Merridi and Lafe's smaller ones, led straight from the jungle out into the open and toward the mountain.

As he stared at it, trying to figure out where the tracks were leading, John realized on some level that the music had changed, and risked popping one of the ear-plugs from his ear for a split second. What had sounded bright and innocuous on the beach now sounded threatening and dirge-like.

John didn't feel the compulsion to follow the sound like his companions had; he had no idea why. Still, they had gone where the music called them, and he was going to do the same until he rescued them or died trying. Clutching his staff hard, he hunkered down to study the mountain and try to figure out where the music was coming from.

At first, the mountain slopes appeared to be deserted. Just as he was getting ready to trot out into the open, John caught a flash of scarlet disappearing into the black. He had to stop himself from calling out – had that been Merridi's cloak he'd seen being swallowed by the dark rock?

Angling around the mountain under cover of the trees, John crept stealthily until he was directly across from the spot where he thought he had seen Merridi.

Sure enough, a broad cave mouth was visible, and men dressed in dark clothing were passing back and forth. He could see no sign of his friends now, but a feeling in his gut told him that they were inside the maw of the mountain. In the distance he could see another bay, hidden from the *Blinkin' Mermaid* as it had approached the supposedly uninhabited island.

Anchored in the bay was the raider's ship.

Those were the raiders, John realized, passing to and fro through the cave's mouth, a shadowy dark slash in the mountain's black rock. The sun was sinking low and, as he continued to slip through the trees for a better look, he noticed that a few torches already flickered from deeper within the cavern. There was something about that dark mouth of rock that chilled him; every bone in his body was telling him *get out of there now!*

John was a light mage. Even though he made use of *unlight*, it was not the same as dark. *Unlight* was different – a turning of the light inside out and back on itself in a way he could *feel*, but not describe. The idea of going down in that dark tunnel, in the absence of light, the idea of those torches going out, one by one, leaving him trapped under tons of black rock, in the dark …

But his friends were in there. He had no choice. He was going to have to use all his wiles and magic to walk right into that tunnel, past all the raiders. Down into the dark to find his friends and rescue them. Finding a spot, he settled down to wait for it to get a little bit darker.

Although John didn't know it at the time, his friends had already been separated inside the cavernous bowels of the mountain. Each had followed the music down a different tunnel, oblivious to the fact that they were no longer all going in the same direction. It was not until the cage doors clanged shut, trapping them each deep underground, that the music shut off with a snap.

Tinker felt like he had been doused with cold water. He came to his senses with a start and grasped the thick iron bars of his prison, shaking them to no avail. Even with everything they had been through since meeting in the Quacker Factory, this was the first time the Corrs had been separated. Panic welled up inside him. "Lafe?" he called out. There was no answer. "Lafe! Lafe!" Still no response. Sinking to the floor, hands still on the iron bars, Tinker waited in the flickering torch light for whatever would happen next.

In another tunnel, Lafe walked into a huge bamboo cage that looked for all the world like something made to hold an exotic bird. When he was all the way inside, the door slid into place and the cage was hoisted up into the air, leaving enough space between the floor and the bottom of the cage that Tinker could easily have fit two or three times. The music shut off and Lafe drew a long, shuddering breath, then looked around him in surprise. "What the *daggers*?" he said, trying to recall how he had gotten there. He remembered being on the beach wit the other Corrs, and then a vague, confused dream about music … hints of the melody still seemed to linger in his ears. The single guttering torch that lit the rock walls that surrounded him went out. Lafe was alone in the dark.

Merridi was under the strongest compulsion of all. Body swaying to the beat, she twisted and shimmied into the depths of the mountain, flashes of dragon scale shimmering across her skin as she went. By the time she had reached a dead end, she was almost entirely dragon, hypnotized, mind blank of everything but the music that she heard. She didn't even notice that she was headed down a steep wooden ramp, into a large earthen pit dug into the floor of the cave, until she stepped off the ramp and the music stopped. Like trying to swim under deep water, Merridi slowly surfaced into reality, just in time to see the ramp disappearing over the edge of the pit. A large iron grate swung into place, with flickering torchlight knifing through the sparse holes. She was trapped.

With twilight came enough shadow for John to be able to summon the *unlight* around him like a cloak. He took a deep breath and stood, studying the cave entrance for one more long minute.

"Looking isn't going to change anything," he told himself sharply. "Quit stalling and get in there."

Putting one foot in front of the other, John ghosted through the men around the entrance to the mountain and crossed the threshold.

At first, there was only one direction to go in, a broad tunnel that arched so high overhead that the ceiling was lost in shadow. John skirted the walls, avoiding the pockets of brighter light created by the torches spaced along the wall. After a while, he noticed smaller tunnels branching off the one he was walking down. Suddenly, the hustle and bustle of men coming and going along the tunnel stopped. John froze, thinking he'd been discovered, then the raiders blinked, looked around them, and resumed their activities. There was something different about them now, though. They were … talking to each other. Prior to the moment when they all stopped, they'd been moving like automatons, John realized. Now they were acting like ordinary men, calling out greetings to each other, laughing, smiling, cursing.

Cautiously, John removed an ear plug. As he suspected, the music had stopped. He kept the ear plug in his right ear in place and held the one from his left in his hand, ready to jam it back in, in case the music started up again. He cocked his head and listened, realizing that he could hear other sounds now that the music had stopped and he could hear again. It sounded like there was a gathering of some kind going on up ahead of him. Even as he strained to hear, one man's voice came to him clearly. Picking up his pace, he moved toward the sound.

After another moment of walking, John stepped into a large chamber carved out of the dark rock. At its center, standing on a platform, was a tall, thin man with a long black beard and ragged black robes. A black flute hung from his waist by a chain. His eyes flashed with sinister fire and a feeling of evil oozed from him. His eyes swept over the gathered crowd and John recoiled, afraid that if those spooky eyes landed on him, he would be seen and recognized for what he was immediately, despite the cloak of *unlight*.

"We have been defeated on the sea today," boomed out the strange man, voice hollow and threatening. "Those who have failed me will be punished!" He pointed with a bony finger, and John realized that not all the crowd was gathered there voluntarily. Those closest to the man on the platform were dressed in raiders' garb and were trussed with ropes. Was that Lafe's father among them? John was almost sure the man was Lafe's dad, but it was hard to tell without a helmet perched on his head.

The man on the platform screamed with rage, and everyone jumped. A hush fell over the room. "Those who failed me will be punished *now*!" he shouted, and a bolt of black light flew from his finger to strike one of the prisoners. The victim screamed in agony as a black, sticky tide washed up his body, freezing him in place as it went. It crept over the top of his head and into his mouth last, so that the scream kept going on and on until long after he had turned as dark as the rock around him. Then it cut off abruptly. There was a stunned silence in the cave.

The dark wizard smiled in satisfaction. His bony hands flicked out to smooth his hair and his ragged robes.

He pointed another finger, and the prisoners cringed. But no more dark fire flew out. Instead, he pointed at the guards. "Take the rest of them away for now. The sight of them sickens me. I'll deal with them later."

The man who had been transformed was left to stand alone, a statue of terror, as the rest of the prisoners were led away.

"Now," said the wizard. "On to more pleasant things. I've captured three new servants today. A young human, a troll, and a dragon. They will all have their uses, I am sure." He held up both hands in a gesture of modesty, as if to deflect cheers that didn't come.

"They are to remain imprisoned, with no food or water, until they have been tamed. You, you and you!" he said, pointing one of those bony fingers. "Keep an eye on them. They are in downside tunnels, in the traps we have set there."

His eyes swept the crowd again. "Now, show me what spoils you have brought me today, those of my servants who have not failed me!"

Men began running forward, carrying bags of jewels and caskets of gold and silver, but John didn't spare them a glance. His eyes were glued to the three men who had been instructed to keep an eye on the newly-captured prisoners, and he darted through the crowd to keep them in sight. Fortunately, the cavern was crowded enough that the occasional bump or jostle he gave to someone in passing went unnoticed. John caught up to the servants just as they left the cavern, and followed them back up the tunnel until they came to a spot where several smaller tunnels jutted off in different directions. One, two, three tunnels. Three friends in desperate need of rescue. The men each grabbed a torch from the wall and hurried down different path. *Choose!* Not knowing what else to do, John headed off after the man who had taken the left-hand path.

At the end of the tunnel, John found a despondent-looking Tinker. His hands were wrapped around the thick iron bars of his cage as if he expected the door to come flying open any moment. His captor settled in a chair with his back to the cavern wall, an oil lamp glowing on the table beside him. "Hey, monster," said the guard. "How's it feel to be the one in the trap? Bet you don't like that, now, do you?"

Tinker just looked at him.

The man stood up and strutted in front of Tinker's cell door. "Yep, tables are turned now. Thought you were gonna come down here and gobble up some tasty human snackage, I bet. But Melore was too smart for you, huh?"

Tinker barely blinked. "Who's Melore?"

"Who's Melore?" The guard sneered. "Only the greatest evil dark wizard that ever lived, that's who! When unsuspecting travelers get shipwrecked or marooned on the island, he lures them into his evil clutches with enchanted music and turns them into slaves who plunder and pillage on his behalf. You're our first troll, though."

"How did you get here?"

"I was on a raiding ship from the frozen north. We were running low on fresh water and laid over on the island to replenish our supplies. One by one, we heard the music and were enchanted. Been here ever since. We attack ships that sail by on their way to Paxia and

Deren. Throw the crew overboard, bring back the ships and all their cargo to Melore."

"You sound pretty happy about it for a guy that's been kidnapped and forced to work for an evil wizard."

Tinker's guard shrugged. "You don't listen very well, do you? I've been enchanted by an evil wizard. I know I *should* be upset. Svetlanda's probably already got a new boyfriend picked out by now."

John was steeling himself to sneak up and knock the guard unconscious when there was a grinding noise in the corner, then a small spray of rubble. From the darkest corner of the cavern, half a dozen warrior gnomes erupted and pointed ungainly-looking cross-bows at the guard. John froze. While he watched, several of them plucked earplugs from their ears.

"You think you can take a troll prisoner and the gnomes of Crystal Mountain will stand idly by and let this happen? They're like our cousins!"

The guard scowled. "You guys again. We kicked your butts a long time ago. Go disappear back down your little holes and leave us alone."

"I don't think so, monster meat!"

The front-most gnome prodded at the guard with his spear. The biggest gnome only came up to John's waist but they were broad with muscle, their fierce faces covered in tattoos, shields and swords gleaming in the light of the oil lamp.

The guard backed up until he was standing next to the cell.

One of the gnomes whistled at Tinker. "Hey, big guy. Snag the keys and let yourself out. Hurry up! We got things to do."

Tinker stood up and grabbed the keys from the guard's belt. Swiftly, he unlocked the door. The gnomes herded the guard into the cell and slammed the door shut.

"Okay, big guy, come with us."

"Where are we going?" asked Tinker.

"We've got tunnels all through this place. Most of us are deaf as posts from all the drilling and exploding we do to mine the mountain, so the enchanted music doesn't work on us so well. Plus, we wear earplugs. Who do you think made all these tunnels?"

"I … I don't know," said Tinker. "I didn't think about it."

"That's what you get for asking a troll what he thinks," said one of the gnomes philosophically. "A whole lot of nothing."

The other gnome shrugged. "My mistake. Anyway, come with us. My name is Togart, and I'm the chieftain of the gnomes of Crystal Mountain. We're the underground resistance. We'll hide you and help sneak you back off the island."

Tinker took a step, then stopped. "I can't."

"Why not?"

"I have friends here. I have to stay and rescue them."

The gnome who had been doing most of the talking looked interested. "Are they trolls, too?"

"No. A dragon and two humans."

"Too bad, buddy. Trolls and gnomes are sort of like cousins – both rock clans, if you follow my drift. I don't think they're as good of friends as you think they are."

Tinker shook his head. "I can't leave without my

friends."

"And we don't do humans or dragons. You alone, or the deal's off."

"I'm staying."

"Suit yourself. We're outta here."

"Wait," said John, stepping out of the *unlight*.

The gnomes stepped back, startled. "John!" exclaimed Tinker happily. He picked the young mage up in a hug that threatened to crack a rib.

"Tinker! Hey, easy on the human!" said John, grinning back at his friend.

"When did you get here?"

John explained that he'd just found Tinker and been getting ready to knock out the guard when the gnomes appeared.

"How did you escape from the music?" asked Togart.

"I don't know, exactly," said John, frowning. He'd had plenty of time to wonder about that, himself. "But I'm a light mage, and I think dark magic doesn't work on me as well as it works on other people. I followed my friends here, then snuck through the caves."

"Do you know where Lafe and Merridi are?" asked Tinker.

"Yeah, I think so," said John. "But before we go rescue them, I have a question for the gnomes. How would you like your mountain back?"

The gnomes huddled in a circle and muttered to themselves for a minute, then turned back to John.

"What would it involve?" asked Togart.

"Taking your underground resistance and kicking out the evil wizard. We'd help. I think if we can defeat the wizard, most of his servants would be glad to be free. Isn't that right?" John turned to the man in the cage.

"Huh? Absolutely! I'd give anything to be back in snow up to my armpits, my big, beautiful Svetlanda by my side, a hunk of roast moose meat in my hand!"

"See?" said John. "Let's free our friends and go kick some wizard butt!"

"Ah, have you seen that thing he does with the black flame? That kind of freezing, screaming torture thing?" asked one of the gnomes.

"Yeah, but I think I can counter that."

"Maybe you should call us when you're sure."

"Come on! Are you gonna be mice or m—gnomes?" said John.

They went into a huddle again, with more muttering. Occasionally, a bearded head would pop up and John would get a squinty look he couldn't interpret.

"Okay, but first, show us what you got."

"What?"

"You know, give us a demonstration of your power. Show us your stuff. That kind of thing."

"Oh. Okay," said John, wondering what on earth he could do.

"Hey, John," said Tinker. "Hit me."

"You sure?"

"What's the good of being half troll if you can't take a hit of magic light once in a while for a friend? Come on, give me a good one."

Concentrating, John held up his staff and let the magic flow. A glowing ball formed at the tip of his staff, illuminating the cavern. The gnomes gave a gasp of amazement.

Remembering what Lafe had taught him about action and reaction, John braced his staff in front of a huge boulder, then released the ball of light. It flew toward Tinker, hitting him in the chest and picking him up off his feet. He flew back through the air and crashed into the cavern wall, making a two foot deep, Tinker-sized depression in the stone. The entire chamber shook when Tinker hit, releasing a fine rain of dust and debris from the ceiling.

Tinker grinned and slowly dislodged himself. "See? John's great!"

The gnomes looked at John, then at Tinker and the big hole in the wall.

"Okay, we're in," said Togart decisively. "What do we do next?"

Chapter Nine

What came next was freeing Lafe and Merridi. With Tinker bent nearly double to fit, they used one of the gnomes' tunnels to slip from Tinker's chamber to Lafe's, leaving Tinker's guard sitting, bound and gagged, in Tinker's cell.

When they got to what looked like a blank wall, Togart stepped forward and snapped his fingers and a door appeared. "Little bit of gnomish magic," he explained. "We don't have a lot, but it comes in handy."

In order to sneak up on the guard, they sent John through to clobber him, cloaked in *unlight*. "Hey, that's pretty nifty," said one of the gnomes, as John disappeared from view. "Can you see out?"

"Of course I can," replied John. "It wouldn't be much use otherwise, would it? It takes a little bit of the color out of things, but that's about it. Otherwise, I can see fine. Just don't ask me to tell the pink pony from the blue one."

"Definitely handy," pronounced Togart. "Okay, get

in there and do your stuff," he said, and shoved John through the door.

To John's mortification, he discovered that he couldn't just sneak up on someone and clonk them on the head with his staff. He settled for sneaking up close, and then quelling the *unlight* so that he appeared to pop into the chamber right in front of the guard's nose.

"Boo!" said John, feeling rather lame. What were you supposed to say to someone in a situation like this?

The guard jumped, then got a better look at John. "Oh, it's just a kid. Hey, there. How'd you get in here? I thought you were one of those sneaky tunnel gnomes for a minute there. Gave me a scare!"

"I'm not a kid," said John. "I'm a mage. And if you don't do what I say, I'm going to blast you into next week."

The guard blinked, then burst into laughter. When he was done laughing, he said, "Okay, kid, that's a good one. Now run along. I've got a job to do here."

John sighed. He'd warned the guy. He pointed his staff and the sun stone began to glow. The guard, looking a little alarmed for the first time, took a step back.

"Hey, John!" said Lafe from his perch above John's head. "Don't forget to—"

John let go the ball of light, and it struck the man squarely in the chest. John flew back through the air and hit the wall, sliding down to the ground slowly.

"— to brace your staff first," finished Lafe.

The rest of the gnomes and Tinker burst through the door and Tinker pounded the guard on the top of the head with one big fist. The guard collapsed instantly. Then Tinker went to pick John up and dust him off while the gnomes lowered Lafe's cage back down to the ground and opened it.

"Hey," said Lafe, hurrying over to where John was wobbling on his feet, Tinker ready to catch him if he fell. "You okay? Thanks for the rescue, by the way."

"No problem," said John, shaking his head to clear it, then wincing. "I knocked out my earplug, though. You see it anywhere?"

"Take some of ours," said Togart. "We always carry spares."

It looked pretty funny, seeing everyone with big plugs sticking out from their ears, but it sure felt a lot safer. John was pretty sure that once the escapes were discovered, the evil wizard would start up the enchanted music again.

They bound and gagged the guard, who was still unconscious, then placed him in the cage and hoisted it back up into the air.

That done, they headed back to the gnomes' tunnel system to find Merridi.

When they peeked out the gnomes' door into the cavern where Merridi was being held, all they saw was a man sitting on the cave floor. They pulled out their earplugs so they could communicate. "Where is she?" whispered John, puzzled.

Lafe pointed at the ground, and John realized the guard was sitting on a huge grate. Before they could decide how to subdue him, Tinker passed them in a crouching run and tackled the guy, who let out a muffled *oof* as he went flying through the air. The guard remained in a crumpled heap as Tinker turned and jerked the grate with both hands, pulling it off the hole and sending it spinning carelessly through the air like an over-sized dinner plate.

"Hey," said Lafe. "Watch where you're throwing that thing!" But Tinker had already jumped into the hole and was boosting Merridi up and out.

Lafe looked at John with a raised eyebrow. "You think he would have been that on-the-spot for us?"

John looked at Tinker, now out of the hole and fussing over Merridi. "Almost. You don't think–"

Merridi looked up and gave Tinker a huge smile as he passed her a pair of earplugs.

"Oh, well. Maybe," John said, answering his own question. "That's … *huh*. Didn't see that one coming."

Lafe clapped a hand on John's shoulders. "Come on, let's go confer with the lovebirds before actual smoochery breaks out. We need a plan more than they need to play kissy face."

"Ah, yeah," said John. *There* was a picture he didn't need in his head. Hurrying after Lafe, John went to talk with his friends.

"Okay," said Lafe, "here's the deal. Does anybody want to just sneak away and leave things the way they are?" John had told Lafe that he thought he'd seen Lafe's dad earlier, and Lafe glared fiercely around, daring anyone to vote to simply escape.

After a moment, when no one raised their hands, Lafe relaxed.

"Alright, then. Now, the wizard is our real goal. Everyone is agreed on that, right?" Everyone nodded their heads. "A lot of the people who serve him are enchanted to some degree, so we want to go easy on them if we can. What we need is a diversion, so that we can lure the guards away from the wizard. That way, the wizard will be more vulnerable to our attack."

"I don't think creating a diversion should be too hard," said Togart. "We've got weapons." He patted the crossbow he carried.

Lafe looked at the crossbow with interest. "What's that thing loaded with, anyway?"

The gnome tilted the crossbow so they could see it was loaded with half a dozen projectiles the size of the gnome's fist. "Mine's loaded with boomers right now – makes lots of noise and smoke, but doesn't do much damage. But we can also fire heavy artillery - explosives that ignite in the air. They do some real damage."

"Nice," said Lafe.

"But even after we get the wizard alone, how are we gonna fight him? I mean, he's a wizard, for *coal's* sake."

All eyes turned slowly to John. He had a brief flash of the inky black magic gunk sliding over the body of the sailor like a tide. Then he squared his shoulders.

"Okay. Okay, I know this part is my job. You guys create a distraction, and I'll take out the wizard." He looked at Lafe. "Don't worry. We'll get your dad back. I promise." *And if we don't*, John thought to himself, *we'll all be inky black statues and it won't matter anyway.*

The explosives were just about set when the music started up again. Along with the music came the sound of men shouting and the clanging sounds of swords being drawn from their scabbards. "They must have realized we escaped!" said Lafe, hastily stuffing his plugs into his ears. The rest of them followed suit.

"Good timing on the earplugs," yelled Togart. "We were gonna need 'em anyway!" Raising his crossbow, he took careful aim with a lit boomer at the furthest charge. The rest of them scrambled to get behind a distant boulder.

There was a long silence, then the sound of a distant explosion.

"That's it?" said Tinker, puzzled.

There was another explosion, then another and another. Pretty soon, it sounded like a handful of winter corn was popping on a hot skillet.

A gnome leaned close. "It's the ear plugs," he shouted. "Makes it seem quieter!"

The tunnel they were hiding in began to shake. The shouts of the sailors and guards began to sound more like panicked yells of alarm. The music stopped, and John guessed that the wizard had put down his flute so that he could shout out orders.

Stealthily, they crept out of the tunnel to peer into the cavern the wizard occupied. Men were streaming from it, chased by the sound of the wizard screaming and cursing them into action.

When the stream slowed to a trickle, and then stopped, Lafe clapped John on the back. "You ready?"

John nodded.

"Don't forget to brace your staff! Good luck, kid!"

"I'm not a kid!" John shouted after him, but it was too late. Borrowed sword held high, Lafe was already leading a charge into the wizard's cave against the remaining guards.

All John had to do was waltz in and take care of the wizard. Gritting his teeth, he stepped forward into the cavern.

A scene of pure chaos met his eyes. Everywhere, the wizard's personal guards were doing battle with the gnomes and the other Corrs. Merridi had transformed into her dragon self and was cutting a wide swath through the crowd, Tinker at her side towering over the gnomes and their opponents. The wizard stood on his platform, eyes flashing, sending out bolts of black fire from his fingertips. His luck was only running about fifty-fifty though. As often as he hit a gnome, he hit one of his own men, and the battlefield was becoming littered with the tar-black bodies of frozen fighters.

John saw him take aim at Merridi and sprang forward.

"No, Melore!" he shouted, in as commanding a voice as he could muster.

The wizard stopped and his black eyes flickered across the room until he spied John, staff in hand.

"You?" said the wizard incredulously. "You are the one responsible for challenging me? You're just a kid!"

"I. Am. Not. A. Kid!" yelled John, as he crossed the room to stand in front of the wizard.

"Ha," Melore said, sounding bored. He waved a hand negligently in John's direction, and a spurt of black flame shot out.

John blocked it with his staff, the sun stone flashing with light as he did.

The wizard's eyebrows rose. "Well, what have we here?" he sneered. "A junior light mage?"

Even as he spoke, two more bursts of dark fire shot out. John blocked them both, then countered with a blazing ball of white light that struck the wizard squarely in the chest.

John went flying backward over the heads of the fighting men. Tinker reached up a hand and snatched him out of the air just before he hit the wall.

Melore bent double with laughter.

When the wizard straightened, he wiped tears of laughter from his cheeks. "Well, well, well. A *very* junior light mage. And not a very well-trained one, at that."

"Brace your staff," whispered Tinker.

John struck the ground hard with the end of his staff, burying it in the hard-packed dirt rubble of the cave floor. He shot another beam of light at the wizard, and this time when it struck, it was the wizard who went flying backwards.

"Good one," crowed Tinker, and slapped John on the back so hard he nearly fell over.

The wizard was rising to his feet, and the look on

his face now was not amused at all.

"Let's see how you deal with *this*," said Melore, throwing his hands up in the air.

The lights went out.

All noise stopped, except for the gasping of men taken by surprise at the dark.

It was the utter, complete absence of any particle of light in the room. John never remembered having ever been in darkness so complete. He felt strange. Almost as if the dark was sucking up his energy. He directed his light power into the staff, willing the sun stone to flair. It gave a weak flutter, then went out. From across the room, John heard the wizard laugh.

"You may not know that dark and light are diametrically opposed," the wizard said with a sneer in his voice. "This blanket of dark will sap every puny bit of light energy that you have. It will weaken and cripple you until your magic is gone, and you will be totally in my power. I will pluck you up and put you in the deepest, darkest cave in the heart of this black mountain, and you will live out the rest of your life in the dark, never seeing the *sunlight* again!"

The darkness crashed in on him. John could feel it like a physical force, pounding at him, wearing him down. Behind him, he heard Tinker breathing.

John fell to one knee. The inky blackness was a weight he couldn't resist.

"John," said Tinker urgently. "Merridi's down here! You have to fight it!"

It was taking all of John's willpower not to fall flat on his face.

There was a rushing in his ears. Over it, he could

make out the wizard's laughter.

"John!" It was Lafe's voice this time.

"John, you can do this! Remember the book? The *History* book! There's raw energy everywhere - in everything! Take it and make it into the light energy you need to fight!"

The wizard must have overheard, because he said scornfully, "Use *wild* energy? He can barely use a staff!"

"How do I do that?" John asked Lafe, struggling to get the words out. It felt like a rock was sitting on his chest.

"I don't know," said Lafe. "But you're a mage. Figure it out! And fast!"

"You can do it, John!" said Tinker.

"You can do it!" said Merridi, a beat later. "I have faith in you!"

Softly at first, then increasing in volume, a chant began in the pitch-black room. "John! John! John!"

The sound made John feel stronger. He staggered to his feet and realized that the chanting *was* making him stronger. It was as if the energy of so many voices was shielding him from the wizard's spell.

In the dark, he tried to imagine each voice as a spark of light, all heading his way, filling his body and replenishing his magical energy.

Somewhere in the cavern, John thought he saw a flicker.

"Keep up the noise!" Lafe shouted. For an instant, John thought he could see Lafe's face.

The chanting grew louder. John pictured the sparks turning into small flames. Coming to him, coming into him, making him strong.

There was another flicker, then another.

The sun stone started to glow ever so faintly. In its light, John could see his hand gripping the staff. He twisted the wood, making sure it was still firmly planted in the ground.

The light was getting stronger. Now he could see each face flickering, turned toward him, as they chanted his name.

Merridi, still in dragon form, tilted her head up to the ceiling and let go with a blast of flame as bright as a comet's tail.

The sun stone flared bright.

In the darkest corner of the chamber, John could see the flash of light reflected in the wizard's eyes.

He gathered up all his power, and a bolt of light flew from the sun stone and struck the wizard. This time, when the wizard went down, he didn't get back to his feet.

Suddenly, there was a flood of illumination; all the torches and lamps that had been snuffed out by the wizard's magic sprang back to life.

There was a moment of stunned silence, then a cheer broke out.

"Quick," shouted Lafe. "Grab his flute and get him tied up before he comes to!"

The nearest gnomes moved to do as they were bid.

The guards that had been fiercely battling them a few moments before seemed to have lost the will to fight. Some were shaking their heads, as if coming out of a daze. Others had simply sat down on the floor, waiting to see what would happen next.

John walked over to a frozen sailor, who looked more like a coal statue than a real man. Touching him briefly with the sun stone, John willed him back.

There was a crackling noise, and the black split and fell from the man, turning to dust before it hit the floor. Dark golden skin reappeared, and the man blinked as if waking from a long sleep.

"Wha— what happened?"

John left the others to explain as he moved around the cavern, turning frozen statues back into living, breathing beings.

"John, that was awesome!" said Merridi, back in girl form, coming over to throw her arms around him and plant a big kiss on his cheek.

"Totally awesome," agreed Tinker, moving to stand beside Merridi.

"Glad it's over," said John weakly, "because I'm feeling a little tired…" Without warning, he passed out cold, right into Tinker's arms.

When John came to, he was propped up against a tree out in the bright sunshine, the mountain somehow looking less somber across the clearing. As soon as his eyes fluttered, Tinker gave a shout. "Hey, he's awake!"

Lafe and Merridi ran over. Behind Lafe, John could see his dad.

"Hey, there, hero," said Lafe. "That was quite a show you pulled off earlier."

"Yeah," said John. "I think I could probably wait awhile before trying something like that again."

"I don't blame you, son. That was quite a feat you accomplished. Defeating the wizard, freeing all of us from his enchantment," said Lafe's dad. "Mind if I shake your hand?"

John stood up, with a little help from Lafe, and held out his hand to Lafe's father. "It's a pleasure, sir," he said, as Lafe's dad beamed and shook his hand hard enough to make his teeth rattle.

"So," said John, when he got his hand back, "what do we do now?"

It turned out that the gnomes had very specific ideas about the next item of business – a huge feast in honor of the Corrs. It was held out in the clearing in deference to both the Corrs and the majority of the wizard's former servants, who had had quite enough of being underground to last them for a long, long time.

"It's fine with us," said one of the gnomes, sighing happily and patting his full belly. "We will take back our mountain again and make it a place of joy once more. We have invited Melore's former servants to stay on the island if they choose and make a life here. Some will, and some desire to return to their homes, or continue on the journeys that brought them within Melore's grasp to begin with."

"What's your dad going to do?" John asked of Lafe.

"He wants to stay here," said Lafe. "He thinks that he and some of the other sailors can turn the bay into a thriving port. They're working out a deal with the gnomes right now for the opportunity to trade the precious metals the gnomes mine in exchange for a small percentage."

"Are you going to stay here with him?" asked John, saying what was on all their minds.

Lafe grinned. "And miss out on what happens next? You must be out of your mind! But once we get Merridi to Deren, I'll probably come back. Now that he's going to be a trader and a merchant instead of a mercenary, he'll need a good salesman on his side."

They sat in companionable silence for a few minutes, watching the people they had rescued eating and laughing.

"Ah, excuse me, but if you've finished eating, we have some business we'd like to take care of," said one of the sailors, approaching the Corrs' table.

"Sure," said Tinker. "What kind of business?"

Togart jumped up on a table and shouted. "Hey! Time for the ceremony!"

Ceremony? John watched with interest as two sailors rolled in a wheelbarrow covered with a gaily covered cloth.

"First," said Togart, "we'd like to present each of you with these small tokens of our esteem, pledges that you will always be welcome here in the shadow of the Crystal Mountain." He then presented each Corr with tough new leather boots and cloaks. Lafe received a short blade with an elaborately decorated sheath, while Merridi received a finely woven new cloak of an even more brilliant scarlet than her original, which was getting rather tattered. Tinker received a swashbuckling leather hat with a long trailing feather, which he delighted in doffing and waving about.

"And now for you, Mage John," said the gnome.

"I really don't need anything," said John. He was getting too much of a kick out of watching Tinker hold his hat in his hand and giving Merridi a deep, sweeping bow.

"Nonetheless," Togart said. When John didn't look at him, he cleared his throat. Loudly. After another minute, he said, "Look, kid, we want to give you this present. It's a big deal to us, okay?"

"I'm not a kid," said John absently.

"Okay, then. Now that I've got your attention, Mage John, the gnomes of Crystal Mountain would like to thank you for ending the reign of the evil wizard and returning our home to us. Therefore, we have conferred and decided that only one gift is suitable to show our true gratitude and warm feelings toward you."

Togart bowed low and motioned for two of his confederates to step forward. Between them, they clutched a plain wooden box.

"You may have wondered how Crystal Mountain got its name," continued the gnome chieftain.

"Ah, actually, I'd been pretty busy up to now. But since you mention it … how *did* Crystal Mountain get its name?" John asked politely.

In answer, Togart took the box and gently opened the lid.

Light shimmered and danced from inside the box. The gnome inclined his head toward John and held out the box.

"Mage John, may I present you a seed pod from the Crystal Tree that lies at the heart of Crystal Mountain."

"You? You are the one responsible for challenging me? You're just a kid!"

Chapter Ten

After the feast, bolts of silk that had been captured by the dark raiders were used to make colorful tents in the clearing. By mutual, unspoken agreement, lamps were left burning brightly throughout the campsite that night. John fell asleep with the light of two moons slanting across the floor of the tent, making the crystal seedpod on the end of his staff sparkle and shine. He had given the sun-stone to the gnome chieftain as a remembrance, infusing it with a soft glow that would last as long as the stone was whole.

They spent two days lolling around, swimming in the surf, eating humongous meals, and listening to Lafe's dad spin yarns about all his exploits as a mercenary. Gnomes, John soon learned, really knew how to eat. While they waited, a small but swift sailing ship was prepared for them. Two sailors were hand-picked by Togart to see the Corrs safely on the final leg of their journey to Deren. They had been chosen partly because they wanted to stay in Deren, and the little vessel could be left there until its rightful owners claimed it. Apparently, it had carried precious cargo for the library at Deren, most of which was still aboard. It had been captured fairly recently and was not yet repainted in the dreary colors favored by Melore. Bolts of bright silk had been used to create a rainbow of colorful sails that gleamed in the light.

As frothy whitecaps danced on the water, the *Bookworm* set sail for Deren.

They were less than a day's sail from Deren when they ran into the storm.

It started out as a cool, bright day with smooth indigo water, but by the time the sun was high, the waves began to churn and soon the small ship was rocking violently. The sailors looked spooked and were muttering to themselves as they made haste to trim the sails and batten down the ship. After everything was as secure as it could be made against the battering waves, one of the sailors manned the ship's wheel and the other climbed the rigging to try and see what was causing the disturbance. Lafe and John stood near the prow, squinting at the sunlit waters and trying to figure out what was going on. "You ever hear of a storm like this – with no clouds and no rain?" asked John, hoping Lafe would say something like, *oh, yeah, happens all the time, kid*.

But Lafe looked just as worried as John felt, and shook his head *no*.

Above them, there was a shout, and John looked up to see the sailor in the crow's nest pointing east. "Braken! Braken! Get us out of here!"

The sailor at the helm hauled mightily at the wheel, but it was too late to avoid the deadly sea creature.

Before John could react, a huge, suckered tentacle rose out of the ocean and grabbed the *Bookworm* in a deadly embrace. The ship pitched, nearly knocking John and Lafe off their feet. The sailor in the crow's nest was shaken from his perch high overhead, and hung on to the mast for all he was worth.

John grabbed his staff and directed a ball of light at the glistening, evil-looking tentacle. It was as big around as Tinker's chest where it came over the railing, and a good twenty feet from tip to where it disappeared into the sea.

The ball of light struck the braken's tentacle, and the injured appendage jerked and withdrew. John sighed with relief.

Too soon! One tentacle had withdrawn, to be replaced by four more, hauling the braken's huge, eerie head with them. The skin of the braken was dead white underneath, the color of a fish that floats belly up on the water, while the rest of its body was covered in a tough, muddy brown hide the color of decaying seaweed. The deceptively soft-looking head held two alien eyes, flat and cruel, and there was a sharp, terrible beak where the mouth should be.

"Fire!" shouted Lafe in John's ear, even as he pulled his new short sword and started slashing away at one of the tentacles. John pointed his staff and fired off a string of light bursts, each one scoring a suckered tentacle with an explosion of light. The braken opened its mouth and made a peculiar, high-pitched gurgling sound that sent chills racing up John's spine. It was like somebody running their fingernails over a chalkboard underwater, but so loud it made the inside of his skull ring. Still, the braken clung tenaciously to the boat, rocking it back and forth.

The sailor overhead screamed piteously. His grip was loosening, all the shaking and rocking of the boat making it hard to hold onto the mast. A few more minutes and he would end up falling into the sea – or into the open beak of the braken, which had just noticed him. John could see its beady, coldly-intelligent eyes look up and fixate on the sailor as he hung in the air. The braken shook the ship again, watching as the sailor screamed and whipped through the air. John could *see* the satisfaction in its eyes.

John leveled his staff and put a shot of light across the braken's beak. The shaking of the ship stopped, and those weirdly flat eyes whirled until they came to rest on John. He walked over to stand boldly in front of the braken, while the grateful sailor scurried down the rigging to a more secure spot. Tinker, who had been wrestling with the big ship's wheel, gave it over to Merridi so he could come stand next to John.

"Yeah, ugly," John shouted. "That was me. And it was me that put those pretty spots on your ugly hide. If you don't want a lot worse, I suggest you let go of our ship, or . . ." John cast about in his head for something sufficiently intimidating to say, "Or the Great Mage John Black will give you a sunburn you'll never forget!"

"What he said!" yelled Tinker at his side.

The braken opened its beak and made a sound suspiciously like a raspberry. The big eyes blinked, and then, without warning, the powerful tentacles released their grip on the *Bookworm* and the monster slid back under the sea. Lafe ran over to the railing to look for it, but the water was as smooth and tranquil as if the encounter had never occurred. Even the waves that had preceded their encounter with the braken had disappeared.

There was a sound behind them. "Ahem," said someone.

John turned. Standing on the deck was a beautiful young water elf. Long blue hair flowed down her back, so long it reached nearly to the deck. Her skin was the calm turquoise of the deep sea when the sun shines on it. A headdress of red coral crowned her head and thick gold bands reflected the light at her wrists and ankles. She wore a golden girdle over a deep purple gown that revealed enough slender thigh to make John have to work to keep from gawking.

"Ahem," she said again, sounding irritated. John glanced over and realized Lafe was lost – his mouth was hanging open, and face flushed as he stared at the gorgeous sea elf in her skimpy gown. Were Tinker's eyes actually crossed?

"Hello," said John. "Welcome to our ship, the *Bookworm*. I'm John."

"I'm Aquella, the water elf. Who are the rest of your companions?"

"This is Lafe and Tinker. That's Merridi up on the bridge."

Merridi, still grasping the ship's wheel, waved with one hand and frowned at Tinker.

The water elf smiled slightly at that, then turned back to John and gave him a cold look. "You hurt one of my pets."

John blinked in dismay. How the blazes had he done that? Had the ship plowed into a cute little dolphin or something?

"I'm really sorry, miss … miss … your Highness," he finished lamely. "I had no idea."

She scowled and stomped a foot. "What do you mean, you had no idea? You pointed that stick at him and *burned* his tentacle! How could you be so cruel?"

"That braken? You're talking about the braken? He nearly killed us! He grabbed the ship, and was getting ready to tip it over! I *warned* him! I think he was going to eat one of the crew!"

She waved a dismissive hand. "He was playing. Besides, braken don't eat people. They eat krill. The whole idea is ridiculous."

"Look," said Lafe, finally getting his jaw to work again. "We were just sailing along here, minding our own business. Your *pet* came along and attacked our ship."

From the look on Aquella's face, it might have been better if Lafe had stayed silent.

"Speaking of *pets*," she said, haughtily, "I heard that you are transporting a dragon across our waters."

"Merridi is no one's pet!" interjected Tinker, insulted.

"Merridi?" Her eyes flashed to the young woman at the helm. "This is the dragon?" She flowed across the deck and up the short steps to the bridge. The two sailors, eyes bulging at the curves revealed by the deep purple gown when Aquella moved, simply stood back and let her pass.

Aquella paused in front of Merridi. "You are the

dragon that fled Krovesport, stowed away on a ship? We have been asked to keep an eye out for you."

John crossed to the bridge. "What do you mean, *keep an eye out for her*? By who? Is that why your braken attacked our vessel?"

In response, Aquella raised her arms over her head and clapped her hands, twice. The sea began to move and swell around the *Bookworm*.

John watched helplessly as a huge wave raised itself up out of the sea and reared over the ship, blocking out the sun.

Instead of crashing on their heads and capsizing the ship, drowning them all, the wave folded over the *Bookworm* like a deep blue lid closing over a pot.

They were trapped in a bubble of air, like the miniature people in a glass globe sold at fairs and markets. Aquella smiled. "See you at the bottom!" she said, and dived over the side of the ship, spearing into the water that surrounded them without a splash.

They descended swiftly through the serene waters. Even though they drew further and further from the sun, a luminous glow permeated the sea, making it easy for John to see the curious fish and other sea creatures that swam around them, often stopping to stare curiously as the ship plunged past them.

In a few minutes, the *Bookworm* was hovering just a few feet over the sandy sea floor. Uneasily, John peered upward, wondering if the huge expanse of water above them was going to come crashing down on their heads.

There was a lurch, and their ship began to travel vertically until it approached a huge rock edifice that looked halfway between a natural formation of rough sea rock and a sumptuous palace. Helpless, the Corrs watched as the ship got closer and closer to the mammoth structure, then entered one of the many chambers that seemed to dot it, as if the *Bookworm* were no more than a child's toy pulled on a string.

The water that had surrounded them disappeared as their ship entered the chamber and they found themselves in a giant rough cavern, docking gently at a wide wooden pier. Aquella waited for them there, a jade staff in her hand, the gold at her wrists and ankles glinting in the ambient light.

Knowing they would not escape this new prison without her help, Lafe instructed the crew to put down the gangplank and the Corrs walked out to meet her.

"Hail," she said, looking amused. "I hope your journey was not too unsettling. While air-dwellers can breath in the water here, they have often have trouble adjusting mentally to the difference for long periods of time. I hope you appreciate the atmosphere we have brought down here for your comfort."

Lafe shrugged. "Would it matter?"

"Unfortunately, no. But come, now. There are many people desirous of meeting you." She turned and walked down the pier.

Exchanging worried looks, they followed.

Aquella's route took them out of the rough chamber where they had docked, and down a long corridor of smooth white stone. The floor under their feet was tiled in intricate mosaics of lapis lazuli, obsidian, garnet and gold. They began to see doors leading off from the corridor in which they walked: huge wooden affairs, beautifully carved, with gemstones the size of John's fist for handles.

Finally, they halted at a set of heavy double doors. The fixtures were made of gold, and the carving in the wood depicted a kingly water lord with a raised trident, waves foaming at his feet. Aquella grasped the doors and flung them open. "They have arrived," she announced to whoever waited inside the door. Stepping aside, she waved the Corrs through.

John gripped his staff and strode through the door followed by Lafe, Merridi, and Tinker. The room they entered was a council chamber. Around a long table sat at least a dozen people. To John's utter astonishment, he recognized Galanoth immediately. The dragon slayer had removed his helmet, and wore a heavy scowl instead. Seated across from him was strange creature who looked like a man, except for his scaled blue skin and tightly folded wings.

Closing the door, Aquella came in and gestured the Corrs to sit on a small platform to the left of the table itself. She then walked around the table to stand behind to several other water elves. At the far end of the table sat a man in a deep blue cloak, his face entirely hidden by his hood. A lock of limp white hair was visible as he turned his head to survey the Corrs. He looked familiar, but before John could figure out why, there was a noise from the head of the table.

An elderly sea elf rapped his staff on the floor,

quieting conversation, and then turned to Aquella. “My name is Eeli. I will be in charge of these proceedings.” He turned and gave Aquella a grave look. “You have called this council, daughter. If all those concerned are now here, I suggest you get it underway.”

Nodding, Aquella stood. “Nearly a month ago, we sea elves began receiving petitions to be on the lookout for a group of travelers. We received a petition from Galanoth, looking for a junior dragon slayer named John Black, who he feared had been kidnapped by a dangerous, shape-changing dragon. He was in desperate fear for his young protégé’s life.” She inclined her head to the dragon slayer, who nodded slightly.

“We then received a request from Cyrus the Dracomancer to be on the lookout for a very special, and vulnerable, young dragoness who may have been kidnapped by a mercenary and a troll.” The scaly blue man with the wings nodded, and John realized that he was looking at the legendary part-dragon, part-human protector of dragonkind.

“Next, Warlic the Archmage asked us to keep a sea-eye out for a young mage, who he heard might be in the clutches of a dark wizard. If we found him, Warlic said, we were to please aid him in any way possible to help him escape the clutches of said evil wizard.”

John realized where he knew the man in the deep blue cloak from – it was the mage who had visited him in the magistrate’s cell in Krovesport, and given him the sun stone as a trinket. The man pushed back his hood and grinned broadly. John was stunned to recognize the young bookseller who had sold him *A Brief History of Magic* so long ago.

"As if that were not enough," continued Aquella, "we then rescued several unfortunate sailors who had been forced to walk the plank. They told us that their ship had been haunted by a group of invisible haunts who had cursed them and then caused their ship to be attacked by a fleet of undead raiders."

One of the water elves snorted, and Aquella smiled. "Regardless of how credible that particular report appeared, it was what we were told. Hard on the heels of that, came yet another story that was hard to credit – a man was found clinging to a sea rock by one of the merpeople. He wore a strange horned helmet, and told her that he had been enslaved to crew on a dark ship, and that the ship had been attacked by the most fearful fighter the world had ever known – deadly with all manner of blades, and that he had defeated their entire crew in single combat and tossed the losers into the sea."

Aquella frowned thoughtfully. "Am I missing anything? Oh, yes – one further tale – this one from a previously unknown clan of gnomes who would now like to open trade relations with the sea elves. They say they had been usurped from their ancestral mountain by an evil dark wizard, who was defeated by the greatest, most heroic troll the world has ever known." She angled her head to give Tinker a measuring look.

"In passing, they mentioned that their champion had received a small amount of help. From a shape-changing dragon, a knife-throwing mercenary, and a light-mage." Apparently finished with her recital, Aquella took her seat.

Eeli nodded. "We appear to have tracked down the

group in question. They consist of a blade-throwing fighter; a half-man, half-troll; a shape-changing dragon; and a young mage. Does anyone dispute that this is the group that has caused such a stir?" The Corrs were subjected to close scrutiny from those around the table, but no one attempted to argue with the elderly elf.

"Very well, then," Eeli continued. "We have been asked to stop, help, imprison and honor various members of this group, and for a variety of reasons, with varying degrees of credibility. I will now open the floor to the various petitioners, allowing you to make a case for what to do with these young … adventurers. Galanoth, as your petition was first received, I will cede the floor to you."

The head of the dragon slayers pushed back his chair and rose to his feet. John tried to catch his eye, but when he did, Galanoth gave him a pitying look, and then turned to those seated at the table. He cleared his throat. "I rescued John Black after his master and his village were destroyed by Akriloth, the fire dragon at the heart of the dragon war. I dropped him off at a nearby village to go in pursuit of Akriloth. Later, when I returned to check on him, a young maiden told me that he had been sorely put upon by the elder in whose care he had been left. I then tracked him to Krovesport, where he was imprisoned by a corrupt magistrate in a home for wayward children. There, I heard, he was enchanted by a dragon and forced to help her flee across the sea to escape her own people, who say she is mad and must be locked away to prevent her from harming those around her. Even her own kind do not trust her! I say, I will take John Black back with me to the home of the dragon slayers, and we will attempt to cleanse his mind of this foul enchantment. The dragon must be returned to her own kind, who will deal with her appropriately." He gave Merridi a murderous look and sat.

Eeli nodded gravely. "Our next petition came from Warlic, the Archmage. Warlic, will you speak?"

The archmage waved a thin hand. "I have little to contribute at the moment, except to say that word had reached my ears of a powerful young light mage whose talent had appeared … unexpectedly. My old friend and fellow mage Qilder had sent me a note saying that he thought the boy's level of talent might eventually exceed his own, and asking if I might be interested in taking over his education at some point. But by the time I was free to come meet him, Qilder had been killed in one of Akriloth's mad rampages and the young mage in question had disappeared. After some searching, our paths crossed again, but he no longer appeared to have the heart for magic."

Warlic's enigmatic eyes studied John for a minute, then he resumed. "It happens, sometimes. The greatest mage can have his heart broken – by loss, by grief, by any of the many vagaries of life. Without heart, the mage loses the spark of magic within himself. There is little for others to do. He must decide to find the spark again himself. I gave the young man what assistance was mine to give. But he had a journey in front of him that I could not walk with him. The next I heard, he had fled with his companions from Krovesport. It sounded as if he might have started to recover his spark. I was interested to see what would happen next, and so I contacted your people to make sure that the spark he had recovered was not snuffed out prematurely by those who sought the dragoness."

The elf nodded. "Cyrus? You petitioned for the protection of this young dragoness, I believe. Would you share your thoughts with us on this matter?"

The blue man rose. "I would be honored. Long have my people been troubled by reports of a hidden clan of dragons tucked far away in the wilds of northern mountains. They are shape-changers, the story goes, and use their skills to lure in hapless travelers to horrible ends. Long have we searched for this hidden nest of evil, but to no avail."

Across the table from him, Galanoth hissed, and it was plain that the mere thought of the shape-changers was enough to put him in a rage.

Cyrus gave him a serene look, then continued. "Then came a report that a young dragoness – and the most powerful shape-changer of all – rejected the actions of her people and had risked imprisonment and death to save a human child who had been captured. Our mission became urgent, to find and rescue her before she was put to death by her own people for her defiance."

Cyrus stopped and smoothed a hand over his silvery white hair. "By the time we tracked her back to her village, she had escaped. We dealt with her clan, and I doubt they will be using their abilities to cause any more harm to unwitting travelers for a long time to come, but we were too late to stop the tracker that had been sent after her. He had been told to kill her rather than let her reveal their secret, and to take out anyone to whom she might have told her tale. The trail led me to the Krovesport Home for Wayward and Abandoned Children."

Galanoth pounded a heavy fist on the table. "Where she met and corrupted my young apprentice."

Cyrus raised an eyebrow. "Where they met, certainly. There our understanding of the story seems to diverge. Our young heroine—"

Galanoth snorted.

"As I was saying, our young heroine was attacked by the dragon assassin sent to silence her. But three champions stepped forward on her behalf, and together the young people escaped on a ship bound for Deren. It was at that point I contacted the sea people on her behalf." Finished, Cyrus resumed his seat.

Eeli sat silent for a long moment, eyes on the table in front of him. John thought that perhaps he had fallen asleep during Cyrus' recital, but the others remained respectfully quiet.

Finally, the elf stirred, and turned his eyes to the Corrs, sitting on their small platform. "We have heard from the petitioners, then. I believe it is time we hear from the adventurers. Young mercenary, I think I would like to hear your tale next."

Before John could react, a huge, suckered tentacle rose out of the ocean and grabbed the Bookworm in a deadly embrace.

Chapter Eleven

All eyes were on the Corrs as Lafe rose slowly to his feet and explained how and why he had ended up at the bottom of the sea in the palace of the water elves.

John was proud of his friend. Lafe was a good speaker, clear and direct and not intimidated by the group he was speaking to. He made it clear that the choices made during this adventure had been his, and not forced on him by Merridi. He described in detail what had happened during the battle between the crew of the *Blinkin' Mermaid* and the crew of the dark raider, and talked about finding his father and helping free him from the dark wizard's enchantment.

After Lafe was done, it was Tinker's turn, and the young half-troll seemed to fill the room as he described how the Corrs had come about, and what happened in the halls of the gnome chieftain. John felt himself blushing when Tinker described what the young mage had done. While Tinker made John sound pretty heroic, he left out all the fear, uncertainty and sheer terror that

John had felt during the actual events. John wondered if doing the right thing really counted if you were totally petrified the whole time you were doing it. If the only thing more terrifying than doing your best was doing nothing at all, was that really heroic?

While John had been thinking about bravery, Tinker had moved on. He was speaking of Merridi now, in such glowing words they surprised John, who had not realized Tinker had such a poetic side.

When Tinker was done, Eeli looked around the table and smiled. "I have little doubt that the young troll has been enchanted by the dragoness; however, I don't think magic has much to do with it. Unless I miss my guess, it's the regular, everyday kind of enchantment of a young man for a young maiden." He nodded his aged head to Merridi. "Now it is your turn, daughter. First, to address any doubters, may we see you transform?"

Merridi drew in a breath, looking uncomfortable, but when Cyrus gave her an encouraging look, she stood and did as she was bid.

It was the first time John had ever seen her transform when they weren't in some kind of crisis; he realized that even in the change, Merridi was pretty and graceful. First it swept her skin, a deep scarlet blush that made her look not unlike Cyrus himself. Then she twisted sinuously as her body elongated and changed; arms drawing into her body, tail winding its way across the tiled floor. In a moment, it was done, and Merridi stood in front of the council in all her draconic splendor.

The silence was so complete that John was sure he could have heard a pin drop – out in the hallway on the other side of the closed doors.

There was a snicking sound, and John realized that Galanoth had eased his massive blade from its scabbard.

"Ah," said Cyrus in an approving tone. "You are as lovely a dragoness as you are a young human. Thank you for allowing us to see you in all your glory, Merridi."

Merridi dipped her great head graciously, green eyes modest. "I would be more comfortable in my human state, if that is alright," she said after a moment. "I feel rather odd being the only animal in the room."

"Of course," said Eeli. "You have demonstrated to our complete satisfaction that you are indeed who you claim to be, my dear. Please make yourself comfortable."

John watched as Merridi changed again, and soon was back in her familiar human form.

Galanoth's sword eased back into its sheath.

Under the council's watchful eyes, Merridi recited the story that John was familiar with. It was kind of funny, he thought. Now that Cyrus was here to corroborate Merridi's story, it didn't really matter – somewhere along the line, John had come to believe absolutely in Merridi's honesty, how she cared about others, about her bravery and commitment to the Corrs and to doing the right thing – which included not eating humans or any other sentient beings.

When she was done, she waited a moment for questions, and when none came, she turned those fabulous green eyes on Cyrus. "Truly, you have dealt with my clan? They will not be hurting or tricking the human travelers any more?"

He nodded. "There were a few," he said with a frown, "who would not accept correction in any form. For them, I am sorry to say, there was a horrific battle, but they could not be allowed to continue as they were. For others of your clan, who immediately ceded to our forces, a more cunning method of being placed in check was devised by my friend Warlic." He was grinning, now, and all eyes turned to Warlic, the Archmage.

Warlic waved a hand dismissively. "It was nothing. I simply made it … difficult for them to catch strangers unaware."

Cyrus laughed out loud. "I don't think they'll be catching anyone unaware for a long, long time, Warlic."

Eeli looked from one to another. "What exactly did you do, Archmage?"

"I bombarded them with an extremely powerful stink spell."

"A stink spell?" said Merridi. "You made them smell bad things?"

"Each other," chortled Cyrus. "It did create a stench that could be smelled miles away," he continued, struggling to control his laughter. "Firmly attached to every clan member, present company excepted, of course. They all stink enough to smell from Deren, and it's not something that can be washed off. Each shape changer now carries its own early-warning system. Anyone willing to get close to something that smells *that* bad deserves what they get!"

There was a harrumph from Galanoth that might have been amusement.

Slowly, all eyes turned to John. He was the only one of the Corrs who hadn't spoken.

Reluctantly, he got to his feet and launched into his story.

When he got to the part about running into Warlic, Galanoth held up a hand to stop him, and turned to the Archmage. "So, you knew of my protégé all along?"

"As I said, Galanoth. I had been contacted by Qilder with the story of an untrained, but very powerful mage who had his magical abilities come upon him suddenly. There seemed no rush at the time. But when I got to Qilder's cottage, it had been destroyed by Akriloth and you and the mage had already departed. I followed you to the village where you left him, and lingered long enough to hang a snout on the greedy councilman who tried to exploit him."

Warlic's eyes, suddenly sharp, shot to John. "You will be gratified to know that he lives in daily fear of your return, Mage John." Warlic's mouth quirked at the corners. "And mine, I imagine. Anyway, where was I? Oh, yes. I finally found him again, wandering about the countryside, but he had no desire to ally himself with another mage at that time. So I gave him what guidance I could, and waited to see what would happen."

"The book," said John.

"Yes, *A Brief History of Magic*, by Stefen Hawks. You still have it, I hope?" At John's nod, Warlic continued. "Good, good. A handy volume, which has just about everything a young loner mage needs to get started. Very valuable."

John didn't point out that it had actually been Lafe who had done most of the reading, or that the book was actually tucked into Lafe's back pocket at that very moment.

When no one else said anything, John continued his story. He talked openly about how much he hated dragons, how his one plan after being caught by the constable in Krovesport was to escape and find a way down to Dunderweed, so he could join the dragon slayers at Smoke Mountain. During this part of his tale, Galanoth leaned forward, both elbows on the table and nodded approvingly. His clear eyes were alight with interest and energy as John described what the school had been like. It wasn't until John explained how he had met Merridi that the dragon slayer frowned.

"And she deceived you about her actual nature?" said the dragon slayer disapprovingly.

"For Lorithia's sake, Galanoth," interrupted an irritable Cyrus, "she was fleeing for her life from an assassin!"

"Just pointing out the facts, dragon boy," said Galanoth. His voice was hot with dislike.

"Please," interjected Eeli. "We are here to discuss the fate of these four young adventurers, and that must remain our focus."

There was silence from both Cyrus and Galanoth, and after a few seconds, Eeli motioned to John to continue. He described how Merridi had – not once, but twice – put herself in danger to save him, and had exposed her true nature to do so. He talked about how his feelings toward Merridi had begun to change, how he'd started to see her as a person – an individual with unique feeling and thoughts and beliefs – rather than as a cardboard-cutout *thing*.

He talked about how their friendship had grown and developed over the time they'd known each other. He described Merridi's heroic role, along with Tinker and Lafe, in all their adventures, downplaying his own.

When he had gotten to the end of his story, he looked at Galanoth. "I haven't forgotten what Akriloth did to my family, my village, and my master. I'll never forget that. But blaming one dragon for what another one has done doesn't make sense to me any more. They're just like all the rest of us. Just because I do something doesn't mean Warlic's to blame for it because he's a mage, too."

"Archmage," corrected Warlic gently, and John smiled.

"Excuse me. Archmage. Just because Krag was a bully doesn't mean that I'm going to be one, too, just because we came from the same place. Merridi hasn't done anything wrong. The only one who's really done anything wrong was me, because I took that man's gold pouch in Krovesport. If you need to take me back, that's fine. I accept that. But Merridi deserves to go on to Deren. And Tinker deserves to go with her. Lafe deserves to get back to his dad. If anyone is at fault here, it's me, and I'll take my punishment. But don't blame the others. They don't deserve it."

John sat back down.

Eeli stood. "And now, it is time for us to deliberate. Shall we send these younglings back to Krovesport to the magistrate? Shall we return Merridi to share in the punishment of her clan? Or shall we allow them to continue on their way? These are the questions before the council."

He turned to the Corrs and bowed deeply. "Your part in these deliberations is done. I ask that you excuse us now. Aquella will see that you receive refreshment and a place to rest while you await the decision of the council. Now, if you will excuse us?"

Aquella stood and led them from the chamber.

They were led to a spacious room, and a table laden with fruits and cheeses and cool carafes of juice and sweet water waited, but John had no appetite. Neither, it seemed, did the others.

Instead, he paced the room, pausing to pull back a curtain and look out the window, somewhat startled to realize that instead of sun and clouds and sky, it showed water and seaweed and fish swimming about placidly. He'd forgotten that they were underwater – his mind had been full of the council meeting. Restless, he turned from the window and began to pace again.

There was a hand on his arm. He turned to look into Merridi's deep green eyes. "John, I wanted to thank you for the things you said in there. You and Tinker and Lafe are the best friends I've ever had. We've come a long way, huh?"

John smiled at her. "Yeah, we have. I can't believe how *angry* I was with you when I first found out you were a dragon. Now I can't imagine not being friends with you."

"Yeah, yeah, yeah," said Lafe, coming over. "You can get all mushy later. You guys think about what we're going to do if the council doesn't vote our way?"

"What do you mean?" asked Tinker.

"I mean, what if they try to send us back to Krovesport? *Daggers* to that, is what I say. We need a plan."

John frowned. "There's not much we can do under here, I don't think. I mean, how many gallons of water are we underneath? That's a long swim, just to get to the surface. And … all my swimming was in a pond back home. I don't think I could swim that far. If we do anything, it will have to be on the way back to Krovesport."

Merridi shook her head. "They're on to us. Once they decide they're going to send us back, they'll be watching for us to make a break for it. And between Warlic and Cyrus, I don't think we're going to be able to surprise them."

"Plus, there's Galanoth," said Tinker, putting a protective hand on Merridi's shoulder. "Even if we get away, if the council decides we should go back, do you think Galanoth's gonna give up just because we take off?"

"The council doesn't represent Lore or anything," pointed out Lafe. "It was just to decide whether or not to let us finish crossing the sea to Deren. Galanoth's got no more authority to stop us than that braken did."

"Which brings us back to my original point," said John. "We have an entire ocean over our heads. How are we going to get back up there?"

There was silence as they all thought. Then Lafe grinned and pulled the *History* out of his back pocket. "Got it! We'll use the *unlight* and *tweak* it a little with some water magic!"

"What?" said Merridi.

"Are you kidding? I don't know any water magic!" said John at the same time.

"Come on, it'll work. You've created a bubble of *unlight* around us before, right? Now just add a little bit of *unwater* to the bubble, to seal us in, and the magic will keep the sea out and the air in – we'll float back up!"

"I can't," said John. "Too dangerous. Way too dangerous. I've never even tried to work with the other elements before. If the bubble bursts underwater, we'll be stranded. We can't risk it. I won't risk my best friends' lives on this. It's crazy."

"Crazier than giving up and going back to Krovesport after we've come this far, just because a bunch of strangers tell us to?"

"Galanoth saved my life," said John slowly.

"So did Merridi, John," pointed out Tinker. "I believe in you. You can do this!"

John looked at Merridi. She hesitated, then nodded her head.

"First, we better see if it works," John said doubtfully.

Lafe picked up a pitcher of water and dribbled a little into John's hand. John formed a bubble of *unlight* on his palm, and focused on feeling *unwater* the same way. He didn't have it quite right at first – instead of moving away, the water just formed a little globe inside the *unlight* and floated there. But with some concentration and a few adjustments, he was able to expand the sphere of water out to merge with the sphere of *unlight* – *and it worked!* The bubble began repelling water as well as it repelled light.

The longer John fussed with it, the more impatient Lafe grew. Finally, he strode over to the door and cracked it open. Like John, the sea elves had apparently not considered that their charges would try to escape from the depths of the sea; there was no guard at the door. "Come on," Lafe said. "The longer we wait, the more likely it is they're gonna finish whatever it is they're doing in there and come back for us. Let's *move*!"

Stealthy, they slipped out the door and down the long corridor, moving as quickly as was possible without breaking into a run and subjecting the tiled floors to the pounding of Tinker's big feet. John wasn't worried so much about the tiles as he was about the noise it would make.

After what seemed like miles of corridor, they returned to the portal through which they had walked to enter the palace from the underwater dock.

They paused, and John swallowed. Then he gripped his staff firmly and called the *unlight*, making the special tweaks and adjustments that would render it waterproof. When it was in place, John looked at his friends. "Are you sure you want to do this?" he asked, still worried.

Tinker grinned and held out a big palm. "Corrs stick together, and Corrs don't get bossed. To the Corrs!" He spit in his palm.

One by one, they all repeated the gesture, and the words. "To the Corrs!"

Walking in time, wrapped in a bubble of *unlight*, they stepped through the portal.

To his great relief, John found that his bubble of *unlight* repelled water as well in the sea as its smaller version had in his hand. He was starting to relax, when another problem revealed itself – how to get it to *go*. They had not given much thought to how the bubble would be moved. It turned out that by synchronizing their movement and all walking forward at once, they were able to direct the bubble through the sea that surrounded them. It was slow going at first, but they soon built up momentum, and were racing merrily through the cavern toward open water.

"You know," said Lafe, rather hesitantly, as they drew close to the egress, "something occurred to me that I didn't think of before we left the dock."

"What's that?" asked John, alarmed by his tone. Was Lafe *worried*?

"Well, the bubble keeps water out, but what if it doesn't let the air in?"

John didn't have time to reply, as they reached the end of the cavern and passed through and into the open sea. The bubble immediately began to rise through the water, although their combined weights slowed the process down somewhat.

Lafe's worry was well-founded, however. They needed to keep the air inside the bubble to make it float, and the trapped air was quickly becoming … *used*. John could feel it becoming less wholesome with every breath. Soon, they were all gasping for air. Gazing through the *unlight* to the surface of the sea above them, it was impossible to guess whether they had a hundred yards to go, or a thousand. He was afraid they wouldn't make it, and was cursing himself for his stupidity.

They were all aware of what was wrong, although they did not speak of it. Suddenly, Merridi grabbed John's hand. "John, can you keep the bubble together if I step outside of it?"

"I … I guess so, but what good will that do?"

"I can transform as soon as I get out of the bubble," she said, eyes shining. "In dragon form, I can help push the bubble to the surface with no trouble. I just need to know that stepping out of the bubble won't rupture it and send the rest of you tumbling out into the water. That will leave more air for you, and get us all there faster. You're sure you can do it?"

John nodded.

"I'll go, too," said Tinker. They all squinted at him. "Merridi, I know I'm not a great swimmer, but I'm awfully strong. That leaves the rest of the air for Lafe and John. I can hold my breath for a long time. A really long time. Let's do it."

Without waiting for John's okay, Merridi and Tinker joined hands and moved through the bubble. Instead of stretching it to keep them safely inside, John let it shrink around them, expelling them with a small pop. Swimming quickly, they shot up and away from the bubble containing John and Lafe.

John sank to the floor next to Lafe, who gave him a weak smile. The floor, John noticed rather dizzily, was completely dry. He felt a moment of satisfaction and hoped fervently they made it to the surface soon. Closing his eyes, he tried to concentrate on breathing shallowly. The last thing he remembered doing was casting a small bubble of *unlight* around his magic book to keep it dry. Just in case.

The next thing John knew, he was bobbing in the surf, soaking wet and with the sun low in the horizon. He shook water out of his face and looked around. Merridi, in dragon form, had a firm grasp on his collar with one clawed paw and on Lafe's with the other. She was using her tail to push them through the water.

Tinker backstroked beside them, grinning, and spewing great spouts of water for the fun of it.

Lafe came to, with a great startled splashing and flinging of his arms and legs, getting water all over John's face again. Merridi looked over her shoulder. "Looks like Lafe forgot one other item in his escape plan!"

"What's that, dragon lady?" asked Lafe, having his momentary panic back under control. "We made it, didn't we? What did I forget?"

All three of them looked at him and gave the same answer. "A boat!"

Far below the sea, although John didn't find out until much later, the council sent Aquella to bring the Corrs back into the council chamber to hear the decision made by its members.

She was gone just a few moments when she came racing back.

"They're gone! They've escaped!"

Eeli narrowed his eyes. "Impetuous! Could they really make it safely up to the surface, though?"

Everyone looked at Warlic. "Possible. Hard to tell with John. His talents are so unexplored. I would think it possible, though."

"See?" said Galanoth, pounding his fist on the table. "You are too soft on them. Against my advice, you have decided to let them continue, and see how they pay you back? They do not even give you the courtesy of hearing your judgment! They run off, determined to follow their own course, regardless of the recommendation of this council!"

Cyrus gave him a thin smile. "I know another who constantly throws aside the judgment of others in order to rush off on his own impetuous course."

"Are you referring to me, you skinny, blue … *dragon*?" shouted Galanoth, jumping to his feet and starting to pull his sword.

Warlic waved his hand, and the sword slid back into its scabbard. The chair Galanoth had pushed aside came scooting back, hitting him in the back of the knees hard enough to knock him back into his seat.

"Kids these days," Warlic said to Eeli. "What are you going to do with them."

Galanoth gave up struggling to rise again, and gave Warlic a suspicious look. "Are you referring to me, or our young escape artists?"

Ignoring him, Warlic rose to his feet. "Assuming they do reach the surface, it's still quite a way to Deren. I suggest that if we don't want them to drown at this late stage of their voyage, we find some way to assist them in getting to shore. Aquella, have you any ideas?"

The lovely sea elf frowned thoughtfully. "There is a pod of dolphins not too far away. I could ask them to help. They've never seen a dragon before, I don't think, or a troll, either. They'd probably be delighted."

"Then make it so, daughter," said Eeli. "And hurry. Warlic is right. I would hate to have them drown now, so far into their journey."

In the water, the Corrs were getting desperate. Merridi was exhausted – even in dragon form, pulling two humans for an extended period of time was tiring, and there was no land in sight. Soon it would be dark, and while John knew a little about navigation thanks to Captain Frolgar, he hated to trust his own sketchy knowledge of the stars to get them safely to Deren.

There was a splash, and Tinker let out a startled

shriek. Even exhausted, the sound of Tinker sounding like a scared little girl made them all look. Tinker was too scared to be worried about how he sounded. He was dog paddling for all he was worth, energy suddenly returned, splashing and heaving in the water. "Something touched me! There's something in the water!" he yelled. "Besides us, I mean!"

Before John could reply, he felt a bump himself and nearly jumped out of the sea. He would have used his staff, but his energy was so depleted he could barely get it to spark, much less function as a weapon. *Bump!* It happened again, then again. Whatever it was, it was rolling him over in the water and he struggled against it, trying to remain on his back where it was easier to keep his tired head above the water.

Bump!

John rolled over, expecting to drown, and instead felt something slip between his arm and body, an object fitting itself into his hand. John felt himself being lifted up in the water – not a lot, but enough so that he didn't feel like he was in immediate danger of drowning.

At that very minute, Tinker went speedily by, towed by two enormous dolphins.

"John! Grab on! They're fish! I think they want to help us!"

Looking at the object in his hand, John realized it was a fin. He grabbed it tightly and, as if realizing that John now understood, the dolphin lifted its snout to chitter happily, then sped up. John turned back to look at Merridi, who had been so valiant, pulling him and Lafe through the water.

"Merridi! Turn back into a human! It'll make it

easier for them to tow you!"

"But where are they taking us?"

"Does it matter?" asked Lafe, calling from her other side. "How much longer could you have gone on for, Merridi, pulling both of us?"

She nodded, and started the transformation. In a minute, they were all cutting through the sea at top speed, buoyed by chattering dolphins, headed for Lorithia knew where. John had a suspicion that it was Aquella's work, and sent her a silent 'thanks.'

Then, remembering the braken, he thought of a better way – maybe. He angled his head to get a better look at the dolphin who was towing him so effortlessly. "Hey, did Aquella send you to rescue us?"

The dolphin nodded its head, sending a spray of water flying.

John wiped his face with his free hand, only getting it wetter.

"Can you talk with her? Now?"

The dolphin nodded again, chittering excitedly.

"And she told you to take us to Deren?" This was John's guess, based on the fact that the dolphins hadn't immediately turned them around and hauled them back the way they had come.

The dolphin made an inquiring noise, as if to say, "Obviously! Now, what's your point?"

"Tell her I said thank you, please," said John.

The dolphin smiled and bobbed its head, apparently liking the idea. Then it turned back to its task of helping to get the Corrs back to solid land.

Chapter Twelve

It was completely dark, and the Zard moon, full and bright, was well up in the sky when they reached dry land. “Where do you think we are?” asked Merridi somewhat shakily, getting to her feet in the shallow water and slogging the last few feet to shore.

John looked around. “I see lights over that way. Looks like enough to be an actual city. Think it could be Deren?”

Merridi studied the lights. “Could be quite a ways off. Half a day’s travel, maybe more?”

Lafe joined them. “I don’t care if it’s the First Feast of Frostvale. I’m not going another step without a fire, food and a good night’s sleep. In dry clothes.”

Tinker, who’d been saying enthusiastic goodbyes to the dolphins, joined them on shore. “I don’t think we have to go that far to get a bed and a bath and a hot meal.”

“You see something I don’t?” asked Lafe.

“When we were coming in, I asked Chuck to take

us as close to where the people were as possible without us being seen. I saw some lights when we were coming in. Should be right on the other side of this little cove here . . ." Tinker walked up to the top of a generous sized sand dune as he spoke.

Lafe looked at John. "Chuck the dolphin?"

John shrugged.

"Hey, just like I told you! Right here! Come on!"

Tinker waved at them enthusiastically and pointed to the other side of the dune.

When the rest of the Corrs joined him, they saw that they were within easy walking distance from a tidy port town where lights burned merrily in tavern windows, and people were still bustling up and down the cobbled streets.

"It looks great, Tinker, but what are we going to use for money?" asked Merridi.

"I could spare an earring," said Lafe, reaching up to ping the ear where half a dozen earrings, courtesy of the grateful gnomes, now dangled.

Tinker jingled a hefty pouch swinging from his belt. "How about some of the gnome gold?"

"Gnome gold?" asked Lafe.

"Yeah, they tried to give me a whole chest full, but it seemed like too much to keep track of. I took a pouch-full. They said they'd hang on to the rest for when we came back."

Lafe looked at John. "Gnome gold. A chest full."

John grinned. "Tinker's right. Too much to keep track of. Come on."

Whooping, he ran down the hill toward the town, energized by the idea of a hot bath and a soft bed. The other Corrs, yelling and skidding on the downside of the sandy dune, were hot on his heels.

They found an appealing inn in short order. The innkeeper had looked a little dubious at the idea of housing someone as large as Tinker at first, but a few gold coins in his fist had persuaded him. Hot baths and clean cloths came first – although Tinker ended up opting for an impromptu wash in the courtyard instead, with two stable boys standing on chairs to pour buckets of warm water on him while he scrubbed.

"Hey," he said cheerfully. "I don't mind. And I can wash my clothes at the same time!"

Soon they were seated at a comfy table in the tavern, drinking ice cold milk and eating hot stew and fresh bread. They heard the latest gossip - Deren was still scandalized by the fact that the current prince, a human, had adopted a Drakel as his son and heir to the throne. The Drakel, who were mammals despite their reptilian appearance, were known for their intelligence, but the locals were still getting used to the idea.

There was a fiddler playing a lively tune on the corner, and fire blazed warm enough to make Tinker's clothes – still damp from their washing – give off faint wisps of steam.

Merridi's foot was tapping to the music and before long Tinker pulled her to her feet. The two of them set off in a lively jig that shook the rafters each time one of

Tinker's big feet came down on the floor.

The innkeeper, looking askance at Tinker's huge bulk sailing gracefully around his tavern, set down a large, tangy biteberry pie in front of John. It was still warm from the oven. John sighed in contentment. Dinner in the tavern and the smell of hot pie reminded him of Qilder, which made him a little sad, but it was no longer the overwhelming, gut-wrenching grief that it had been right after Akriloth had destroyed everything.

He knew he'd miss his parents for the rest of his life, and he still hated Akriloth with a strength that surprised him sometimes, but it no longer eclipsed every good thing that had happened to him.

"Come on, John, let's dance!" said Merridi, grabbing his hands. Before he knew it, he was swinging through the steps of a country jig, just like he used to do at home.

He looked over his shoulder and saw Lafe dancing with a pretty, red-headed barmaid, his golden earring glinting in the light. Tinker was dancing with the innkeeper himself, a large, rotund man whose huge girth was easily dwarfed by Tinker.

After a few minutes, John begged off, laughing, and returned Merridi to Tinker's capable hands. "I'm too tired," he said. "We swam halfway across the sea today! You've got to cut me a little slack!"

An hour later, they walked to their rooms – John lighting the way with his staff – and fell into soft beds with clean linen and thick blankets. "A pillow!" he noted drowsily to himself. "How long since I slept with one of these?"

He fell asleep before he could think of the answer.

The next morning, they were up bright and early. After eating a hearty breakfast – also hot – they caught a ride on a peddler's wagon into the city of Deren.

It was a vast, sprawling town, full of white stone buildings set like gems on gentle, rolling hills. Gardens abounded, fall flowers spilling out abundantly. They decided to use a couple more of Tinker's gnome coins to buy fresh clothes and spent a couple of hours wandering the marketplace, admiring all the trinkets and finery they found there.

They ducked into another tavern for lunch and a place to change into their new clothes, and John was amazed when he saw Merridi, green eyes shining with delight as she twirled her brand-new, bright red skirt. As she moved, matching ribbons flew out from the soft, dark clouds of her hair. She had actual shoes on her feet instead of scuffed boots, and a soft white blouse set off her rosy skin.

"Wow, Merridi! You look like … a *girl*!" said John, with more enthusiasm than tact, but Merridi just laughed and gave her skirts another twirl.

"I know, huh!" said Tinker proudly. "But not like a girl – like a lady. A fine enough lady to be accepted into the finest school in all of Lore!"

"Yeah, but only if we get her there sometime this century," said Lafe, sounding bored. His eyes were twinkling though, and John knew he was just as excited as the rest of them about finally getting Merridi to Deren's famous School of Thought.

"I guess you're right," said Merridi. "It's really time to go, isn't it?" There was a hesitation in her voice that made John look at her sharply. Her eyes were on Tinker, and suddenly John understood. When she had first said that she wanted to go to the School of Thought, she and Tinker barely knew each other. Now, though, things were different.

If she got accepted into the school, what would Tinker do? Hang around Deren while she studied? And – here was a really shocking thought – what would he and Lafe do?

John had never considered that. What *would* they do once Merridi was safely established in Deren?

Before he could think about it too hard, Tinker clapped him on the shoulder. "Let's get this done," he said, smiling. "Forward, Corrs!"

The School of Thought sat on a large green hill outside of Deren. It was composed of a number of different colleges, each in its own sparkling white building, with paths that led to and fro throughout the grounds.

After asking two white-robed students they encountered by the gates, the Corrs headed for the main building, which sat in the very middle of the complex.

It was surrounded by shady trees and broad, cobbled pathways, and above the enormous open front doors was carved a set of runes. "In Knowledge is Freedom," Merridi translated solemnly.

"Ah, very good!" said a merry voice from behind them, and John turned to see a small moglin in a mulberry-colored robe. "You are an excellent translator," the moglin continued cheerfully. He sported a pair of thick glasses and an intricate tattoo on one arm, and John took him for a student, which was surprising. Moglins, a small, lighthearted race that proliferated throughout Lore, were noted for many things, but intellect wasn't usually one of them.

They were excellent healers, generally cheerful, helpful and generous to a fault, with elongated heads and big ears atop small, furry bodies. They were naturally inquisitive, but not inclined to anything that demanded lengthy commitment or hard work.

On the other hand, John thought to himself, he'd just learned that he couldn't judge every dragon by the actions of one. Was it any fairer to judge one moglin by another?

This moglin looked slightly overburdened. He clutched several books in one hand and carried a large staff in the other. John moved to take his books before they toppled out of his grasp.

"Thank you, strangers. I just came from the library and grabbed more than I could carry. I go by the name of Mongo some days, and today is one of those days! Who might you be?"

They introduced themselves one by one. The moglin listened gravely, then shot Merridi a curious look. "And you, learned scholar of the ancient runes – have you come to apply for a teaching post? I was unaware that there were any new teachers being sought at the moment, although there is much that happens here I don't hear about – at least, not by *intent*."

John doubted that. The moglin might be wearing glasses as thick as a Zard's hide, but John was willing to bet the rest of the gnome's gold that very little escaped that sharp glance.

Merridi sighed. "No, not a teacher, nor much of a scholar at the moment. I've come here to apply to the school, to see if I could gain admission as a student."

Mongo looked thoughtful. "I believe the headmaster is out at the moment. And I would know, as I keep his appointment book. Would you like me to show you to a chamber where you may wait? It was just about time for my mid-afternoon snack. Are you in the mood for some cool fruit juice and cookies? We can talk and you can tell me your story, and maybe I'll be able to help you find a way to impress the headmaster when he shows up. Terribly hard to impress, he is. You'll need a good story to catch his interest."

Merridi looked at the rest of the Corrs and nodded. "We'd love to visit with you while we wait for the headmaster."

"All of you?" said the moglin dubiously, peering up at Tinker from behind his thick glasses. "I'm going to need more cookies. Ah, well. Follow me." And waddling up the steps, he led them through the doors and into the School of Thought.

When they arrived at their destination, a cozy chamber with plenty of cushy chairs for all of them, the moglin took his books and set them on a far desk, then bustled about getting platters of cookies and glasses of sweet juice for his guests. When he was done, he hopped into a chair and selected a cookie with a sigh of satisfaction.

"That's good," he said, beaming at them all. "Now, tell me how you got here, while we enjoy our snacks."

Once again, Merridi launched into her story, but this time it was fun, with the moglin supplying appropriate expressions of horror, amusement and surprise to each part and the rest of them chiming in with details whenever they felt something important had been left out. It sounded different when they weren't trying to impress someone, and the moglin was a great listener. John hadn't laughed so hard in … he couldn't remember the last time he had laughed like that.

Finally, they were done, and John glanced up at a wall clock, shocked to realize that over an hour had gone by while they regaled their host with the story of their adventures.

"Hey," he said, pointing at the clock. "Shouldn't this headmaster guy be back soon?"

"Ah, headmaster, schmeadmaster," said the moglin, waving a dismissive hand. "He's a lazy rogue. He'll be here when he gets here."

Then the moglin sat forward and looked at Merridi intently. "But, seriously. I've listened to your entire tale, my dear, and I'm still not convinced that the School of Thought is where you belong. If what you're truly seeking is a safe haven where you can be yourself, there is a village of peaceful dragons in Corelith where you could be among your own kind and be free to be yourself. No one would look at you twice if you went there."

"A village of peaceful dragons?"

"A village composed of all kinds of peaceful creatures – artists and dreamers, peacemakers and scribes," said Mongo. "A wonderful place for someone trying to escape from the trying times in which we live."

"Do you think they would accept me?" asked Merridi, clearly startled.

"Oh, I'm sure of it, my dear. Just think. You could have a home of your own, a place where you fit in, where everyone was like you are. Wouldn't that suit you better than hanging out in some dusty old school with a bunch of dusty old professors?"

"It sounds wonderful," said Merridi slowly, "but I don't think that it's for me. If I learned anything in the last few months, it's that hiding away somewhere, isolated and alone, surrounded only by people just like you – it just leads to stagnation and arrogance. Look at my people. They had stopped thinking that anyone mattered but them. I don't want to be like that. I want to learn all about other people, other cultures, all the different ways the people of Lore live their lives. And eventually, I want to travel, to see them all for myself."

"Hmm," said the moglin. "A student of culture. That sounds like our anthromorphology department, if I do say so myself."

"What's anthromorphology?" asked John, stumbling slightly over the unfamiliar word.

Mongo pushed his glasses back up his nose and looked at John. "The study of shape-changing and shape-changers, of course! I hear they might be looking for a few good advanced students to travel the known world and document who and what is living in the hidden byways of Lore."

He hopped down from his chair and began clearing away the platters that had been piled high with cookies not so long ago. "But what about the rest of you? Where will you go? Was your task just to drop off this charming young future scholar and skedaddle? Or do you, also, have yearnings for erudition?"

"I'm not exactly sure what that means," said Lafe, "But I'd like to learn more about business. My father just started a trading company, and I have a feeling it's going to go big. Do you have a department that teaches things like that?"

The moglin smiled. "You just happen to be in luck. Not only do we have a department of financial transmutation, but we also offer an undergraduate degree in shurikenology. You'd be surprised how well the two go together."

The moglin turned to John. "And you have a yearning to learn more about magic, I bet. The science of the art. It would be an excellent course of study for one of your talents."

John frowned. "Kind of. I mean, I'm interested and all, but if I had my choice of anything, I think I would like to learn more about how to help different kinds of people live together in peace, while respecting each others differences. Does that make sense?"

The moglin's eyebrows shot up. "A political career? You have managed to surprise me. We do, however, have a school of politelekinetics to which you might apply with good result."

John shook his head. "I'm not sure what poli-tele whatever you said is, either."

Mongo smiled. "A course of study which combines

politics, explosives and mind over what matters, young man. We used to offer them separately, but so many students who took one took all of them, that it was easier just to bring them all together into one department."

The moglin turned to Tinker. "And you, sir? Have you aspirations of an educational nature? Will you, too, astound me with an unexpected talent – for poetry, perhaps, or painting?"

"No," said Tinker, laughing. "I just want a chance to stay with Merridi. If she wants me too, of course. But I like flowers, and I notice you have a lot of gardens around here. Maybe I could get a job taking care of the flower beds – you know, raking, tilling, planting, watering, feeding them little bugs. Stuff like that. You know of any openings?"

The moglin shook his head. "Unfortunately, no. The grounds are all maintained by students of the school of horrorculture – don't pick the roses, or they might pick back! – but if you have a knack for greenery, they might consider taking you on. Something to think about, certainly. If, as you said, the young lady is amenable to your continued presence."

Merridi blushed, and so did Tinker. "I, ah … Tinker, of course I want you around!" Her hand stole into his, and they looked into each other's eyes.

"Okay, here we go again with the schmoopery," said Lafe, sticking an elbow into Tinker's ribs. "Look, this is all nice and good, but it doesn't mean anything until the headmaster says so, and I don't think he's going to be as easy to convince as you are."

The moglin blinked. "What do you think it's going to take to convince him, then?"

Lafe shrugged. “I don’t know, exactly. Tests and stuff, I bet. Entrance exams? Yeah. That’s it. Entrance exams. Grades. That kind of stuff. How can you work here and not know this junk?”

The moglin made a tsking sound. “You’re absolutely right. What was I thinking of. Actually, I have a set of entrance exams right around here somewhere. You can get started on them while you wait. Let me see. Where on earth did I put them?” he muttered to himself, banging drawers, until he uncovered a small safe that had been almost buried by books and papers.

He fiddled with the knob on the front for several minutes, before blowing out a frustrated breath and turning back to the Corrs.

“Are any of you any good with puzzles?” he asked. “The headmaster has the safe set to only open if you can answer three of his puzzles, and I can never remember the answers.”

“What kind of puzzle?” asked Tinker with interest.

“Oh, some kind of math thingy,” said Mongo, waving a hand. “Cookie-making is much more my line.”

“If it’s math, Lafe’s your man,” Tinker said. “Go give him a hand, Lafe. You’re better with numbers than all the rest of us put together.”

Lazily, Lafe rose to his feet and walked over to where the moglin waited by the safe. John followed, just to see the puzzle.

“See here?” said the moglin, indicating a chart on the front of the safe. “Answer this question, and the number you get is the first number of the combination.”

John looked over Lafe’s shoulder. In a watery green window, he saw a question slowing floating past:

If 6 and 2 is 24,
8 and 5 is 52,
2 and 7 is 9,
10 and 2 is 60,

Then what is 4 and 3?

"Simple," said Lafe. "Each answer is the sum of the two numbers multiplied by half the first number. The answer to the last one is 14."

The moglin spun the dial to the correct number, and there was a snick as the tumbler clicked into place.

"What's the next one?" asked Lafe.

As if it had heard him, a new question, followed by a series of numbers, formed in the window:

What is the missing number?

|9 2|1 4|3 8|
|5 1|9 3|4 2|

— — — — — — —

|1 8|3 5|2 7|
|2 6|? 1|5 3|

— — — — — — —

|6 1|5 2|7 4|
|7 3|4 6|1 5|

"The answer is eight," said Lafe confidently. "The sum of each block is 17. And 3 + 5 + 1 = 9, subtract 9 from 17 = 8."

The moglin entered the number and there was another click.

"Last one," said John.

Obligingly, the question changed.

What is the next number in the series?
1 3 6 10 15 21

"Twenty-eight, right?" said Lafe.

"How'd you come up with that?"

"It's the simplest one of them all," Lafe replied. "You just add a number that increases by one each time to the running total."

"Huh?" said John.

"Like this: $1 + 2 = 3$; $3 + 3 = 6$; $6 + 4 = 10$; $10 + 5 = 15$; $15 + 6 = 21$; $21 + 7 = 28$. Like I said. Simple."

"Right."

The safe popped open, and the moglin extracted a sheaf of papers. Triumphantly, he turned, waving the entrance exams. "Now, just let me find some scratch paper and quills and ink, and you can get started."

A cold sweat broke out on John's forehead. "I … I'm not ready for this. I really didn't think…" he looked at Tinker and Lafe, who appeared just as flustered as he felt.

"Nonsense," said the moglin cheerfully. "No time like the present. By the way, light this lamp for me, would you, John?"

Obligingly, John flicked a tiny spurt of light at the lamp wick, which glowed cheerily. The moglin nodded his approval. "There's a handy trick."

He passed each of them a folder marked 'test'. "Now, hurry up, so you can have these done before the headmaster shows up."

Dutifully, John opened his folder. Words swam before his eyes. Frowning, his lips moving silently as he read, he got to work.

An hour later, a chime sounded softly. "Ah! said the moglin. "Time's up! The headmaster will be here any moment!"

John looked up desperately. "I'm not done yet! I'm still trying to figure out the first question!"

"Tut, tut, no complaining," said the Moglin. "You're the one who wanted an entrance exam."

"No, I didn't," said John indignantly. "He did!" He pointed at Lafe, who was still muttering to himself as he tried to do long division in his head.

"Wait," said Lafe, trying to pull his paper back out of the moglin's hand. "I'm almost done. If I divide four warehouses full of eighty crates of Taladosian metal-work each by sixteen markets in three different cities . . ."

"No extra *time*," said the moglin forcefully, yanking Lafe's paper away.

John looked at Tinker, who was sitting serenely in his chair, and Merridi, who was holding her paper out for the moglin to collect.

"What's the matter with you guys?" demanded John. "Why aren't you going all super-zard over this? That was awful!"

Merridi looked at him, surprised. "Mine only had one question. I didn't really have to think about it. I just hope the headmaster agrees with my answer. Tinker?"

He bounced in his seat, making it creak alarmingly. "Mine was easy, too."

Before John could ask him what his question was, there was a rap at the door. A drakel with thick brown hair stuck his head in.

"Ah, Nel, old friend. Are these the new students you said were arriving, then?"

The moglin waved the test papers at John and his friends. "Yes, they are, Prince Tralin."

"Prince?" John sputtered, jumping to his feet.

"Yes, but there's no need for that. We're much less formal here in the School for Thought than at the royal court. Correct, Headmaster Nel?"

"Headmaster Nel?" asked Merridi, blinking at the cheerful moglin who had offered them juice and cookies. "I thought you were Mongo, the headmaster's secretary."

The moglin sighed and picked a battered scholar's hat up off his desk. "I guess it wasn't a Mongo day after all. But I do keep the headmaster's schedule," he said with an impish smile. "I just didn't mention that the headmaster's schedule was *my* schedule. Now, I suppose it's time to put my headmaster's hat back on. I take it off every day from two to four." He settled it firmly on his head and sighed. "There we go. School is back in session."

The prince took a seat in one of the chairs and motioned for everyone to sit back down. "And I suppose all the cookies are gone as well?"

"I think I might have saved you one or two," said the moglin, retrieving yet another platter piled high with cookies from a cabinet door.

The prince looked at the Corrs with satisfaction as he nibbled a cookie. "So, how was the enrollment process? Speedy yet helpful, I hope."

"I … we haven't enrolled yet, Sir," said John. "We just finished our entrance exams. I don't think I did very well on mine, honestly."

"What's this? Entrance exams? Is that something new?" asked the prince with interest.

"Well, they seemed to expect it," explained the moglin. "I didn't want to disappoint them." They each received a test based on their expectations."

John gave Tinker a suspicious look. "Tinker, what was your test?"

Tinker looked vaguely astonished that John would ask. "Didn't we all get the same one? Mine said, 'what's the most important - the rose or the weed?'"

"And what was your answer?" asked the moglin with interest.

"They're each the most important, to themselves," said Tinker.

When everyone just gaped, he shrugged. "Plants have feelings, too, you know."

Lafe smacked himself in the forehead. "I had twenty-seven pages of math."

"And you made an effort to answer," said the moglin. "That's what counts."

"I had an essay question on the conversion of wild mana to controlled magical energy," said John. "I think I probably knew the answer, but I didn't have enough time to finish reading the question. It was thirty pages long."

The moglin grinned.

The prince turned to Merridi. "And what was your question, my dear?"

She looked thoughtful. "What is life's greatest treasure?"

"And your answer?" prompted the prince gently.

She turned her great, green eyes on him. "Friendship."

"Ah," said the prince, with immense satisfaction. "Nel, as usual, you have chosen our new students wisely and well." He stood, and the Corrs all rose to their feet, but he waved them back down. "Now, I must go attend to some princely business or other. But I've enjoyed meeting you all very much, and I'm looking forward to seeing you about campus. Congratulations on your admission to the School of Thought."

He made his way out the door, pulling it quietly shut behind him.

The moglin sat on his chair, swinging his small feet. "Well," he said, when they all turned to look at him, "I guess I should show you to the students' quarters." He hopped down off his chair.

"Wait," said John. "That's it? How do you know we really qualify? What if I get in and I can't do what you think I can?"

The moglin gave him a surprised look. "How did you light the lamp I asked you to?"

John shrugged. "I don't know. I didn't really think about it. I just … called up a little light, and sent it out to the lamp."

"Exactly. Extremely sophisticated magic. No spells or conjurations. Pure conversion of raw mana into light. I'm satisfied."

He turned to Lafe. "And you handled a complex mathematical instruction without even thinking about it. You'll do."

"The test? I was worried that I was kind of slow. But a lot of the problems were kind of new to me.

What's an integer, by the way? I've never heard that word before."

The moglin waved a hand. "You'll end up learning a lot about integers before you get out of here, I'm afraid. But that wasn't the test. The real test was taking a large bundle of paper and dividing it up according to instruction. That, you excelled at."

"Was my test a fake, too?" asked Merridi. "Mine and Tinker's?"

"Oh, no, my dear," said the moglin gently. "Yours was the most important test of all. I had to know what you had learned from all your experience. You are truly wise, Merridi, as is your large friend. You Corrs are a lucky bunch to have each other, and it's lucky that we here at the School of Thought have you."

They followed him out the door and back to the entrance of the building. "Now let's see. Where did they put those dormitories?"

Chapter Thirteen

It had been nearly a month since the Corrs arrived at the School of Thought in Deren. Lafe's father had come to visit and had been duly impressed both by Lafe's plans for future expansion of their blossoming trade empire, and by his new skills with the small but deadly shuriken.

Warlic had come out once already to be a guest speaker at the college of magical arts, and assured John that while Galanoth was still somewhat miffed that he hadn't been able to skewer Merridi on the spot during the council meeting, he had plenty of other *violent* dragons to keep him occupied, and was well on the way to forgiving John entirely for opting to become a peacemongering mage rather than a magic-wielding dragonslayer.

Tinker had assumed his role in the school of horrorculture with enthusiasm, and the dean was happy to turn to the thick-hided half-troll whenever a prickly problem developed.

"So," Merridi said one evening, when they were all relaxing in her room, "if everything's going so great, why do I feel so…"

"Bored?" said Lafe.

"Stuck in a rut?" said John.

"Sick of the same-old, same-old?" finished Tinker.

"Yeah, exactly!" she said. "You guys, too?"

They all nodded. "Don't get me wrong," Lafe said. "School's cool and all, but I could use a little … action, I guess."

Just then, there was a knock on the door.

"Come in," called Merridi.

A young drakel woman stuck her head in the door. "The headmaster sent me to— oh, good, you're all here together. That'll save some steps. Anyway, he sent me to get you. He said you have five minutes to pack a bag and get to his office."

John jumped to his feet. "Did he say why? Are we getting kicked out or something?"

The drakel woman shook her head. "No, nothing like that. From what I gathered, a small war broke out when a trade deal between the Darkovian vampires and the farmers of Granemor fell apart. Seems a shipment of seed-spitters escaped, and now the plants are roaming all over the country-side, spitting seeds at anything that moves. The whole populace is in an uproar, and the vampires and the farmers are arguing about who's responsible for rounding them up and paying the damages. Headmaster Nel wants the four of you to go there and … *do* something. He mentioned a … *field trip*? Oh, and you might have to fight your way through a bunch of evil undead to get there."

Grinning, John reached for his staff. "Did I say I was *bored*? What was I thinking?"

"Hey, kid," said Lafe, tucking shurikens as well as more conventional blades into every pocket and fold of clothing he could find.

"I'm not a kid. What?"

"You know what the mercenaries say back at home when the adventure is about to start?"

"No," said John, interested. "What *do* they say?"

"Battle on!"

Afterword

While others may swing a sword with great effect, garnering gold and glory through their heroic deeds, it has been my humble lot in life to wield a pen. I am well-satisfied with this role - I may never know the exhilaration of battle, but neither must I sleep on hard ground or march miles on an empty stomach to achieve my goals. At the end of a hard day of scribing, a hot bath and a soft bed always await me. But even those of us who merely keep the home fires burning have duties and responsibilities, and recording the history of Lore for future generations is mine.

Barely out of the egg, my mother used to keep myself and my clutchmates entertained with tales of the great heroes of Lore. Now that I am grown, I wish to do my part. So I have taken it upon myself to become a chronicler of Lore's newest heroes, whose deeds have not yet become legend. They will carry the banner of Lore into a glorious future.

I hope you have enjoyed the story of John Black and his friends. They never thought of themselves as heroes, never thought of their adventures as the stuff of legend. But they faced and fought evil in many forms, chose friendship and honor over their own safety and security, and learned some hard lessons in so doing. Could any hero say more? Were the rewards worth it? I look forward to hearing your opinions of my tale.

Lyra Trice Solis is the author of three novels, has six wonderful children, and a doctorate in clinical psychology. In 2008, her oldest son was an avid player of AdventureQuest, the first game made by Artix Entertainment. After watching him play, Lyra decided to make a character of her own! When she read a post on the official forum discussing how quests are written, Lyra put pen to paper and wrote one herself. The team enjoyed it so much that she was almost immediately invited to join AQ's writing staff!

She contacted Galanoth, AdventureQuest's Creative Lead, about doing a novel based on the game. He agreed to review three story proposals and accepted *The Dragon's Secret*. Inspired by the game's storylines, Lyra immediately set to writing and with the help of her fellow staff members, began to see her vision come to life in the form of *The Dragon's Secret*. She calls it "an amazing moment for this writer, fan, and player! AdventureQuest isn't just a game – it's a team and a family which has made me feel so welcome, and given me a great opportunity."

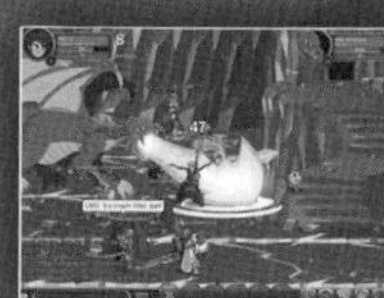

AdventureQuest WORLDS
New Character